Crisis Core: Final Fantasy VII Reunion Complete Guide

Ernest Morin and Curtis Sims

ISBN: 979-8-3696-5652-5

CONTENTS

Crisis Core: Final Fantasy 7 Reunion is one of those remasters that will likely be played by newcomers and returning veterans in equal measure. The original Crisis Core, after all, came out for PlayStation Portable — a modestly successful handheld in the West, perhaps, but hardly a big enough deal for every Final Fantasy aficionado to have given the game a try.

Crisis Core is sure to be a hit with gamers, and luckily, those gamers have a place to come for help. Our complete Basics section will get you up to speed on all of the nuances of the game, while our Walkthrough and Missions section will get you through the toughest spots anywhere in the game. Our massive Appendices section outlines each item, accessory, piece of materia and more. Basically, we have an incredibly useful resource for all you PSP-wielding gamers.

TIPS AND TRICKS

General Tips

There is no Chapter Select in the game. While Final Fantasy VII: Remake has one, both the Reunion remake and original PSP versions of Crisis Core do not. This means that unless you take advantage of your save slots, it will be completely impossible to return to an earlier point in the story without restarting the entire game. This is especially important for those wanting to get all Trophies / Achievements in Reunion!

Save often! Every time you approach a new Save Point, or make significant progress you should save your game. This helps out especially in Reunion, where there are Trophies tied to the various minigames that you only have a limited window to attempt.

That said, also keep in mind that Reunion only has 30 save slots! This is not an issue on PSP, where you can have as many saves as you have space for on the Memory Stick.

Get everything in the story missions! You cannot return to any non-side quest Mission location by the end of the game (since there's no post-game state), so anything you miss will be lost forever eventually!

If an object or character has an orange interact prompt, that means it will unlock a new Side Quest, Mission or Minigame you haven't tried yet.

There's a woman on the ground floor of the Shinra Building who sells free drinks. Normally the first one refills Zack's health, but if Zack is already at full health, he'll get the Raise status, which means he'll revive after being killed! That's effectively a free Phoenix Down!

Talk to everyone! Particularly in Midgar, there's many people you can talk to who will unlock things such as email addresses, side quests to participate in, and even new side quest Mission chains to try out at a Save Point. These will change after every Chapter too, so make sure to do a full sweep of Midgar every time you visit.

There is a mid-game point of no return. After Zack returns from Junon, he'll have to talk with Kunsel in the Shinra Building to progress the story. Make sure you've done everything you want to in the hub areas before doing this!

While there is a New Game + feature, accessing it isn't intuitive: you need to make a Save after watching the post-credits cinematic, then go back to the main menu and load that save.

Combat Tips

Proceed with caution! Generally speaking, after a Chapter has concluded (marked by a screen of a character accompanied by the Crisis Core logo), the enemies in the next Chapter will be stronger than what you've faced thus far. Because of this, don't run into them unprepared: level up a bit with the side quest Missions and make sure you're stocked with the items you need.

If you want to avoid random encounters (particularly during optional Missions), hug the walls to go around the edges of the combat area. This can be rather helpful for side quest Missions if you can only really handle the single, tough fight at the end.

That said, don't avoid battles all the time! You get gil, SP and XP for defeating enemies, so avoiding battles frequently will mean you'll find yourself underleveled as you progress through the game.

Use MP sparingly! You'll always want to have some MP in reserve, since Cure will be a regular spell to use, and some of the most useful Materia spells will also consume the most MP. You don't want to be spamming Fira only to be caught with no MP to heal yourself when you need it!

All Materia, be it Magic, Command, Special or Support Materia, will have a short period where Zack has to stand still to perform it. Zack will be completely open to attack during this time, so make sure to get Zack out of danger at the right moment to make the most of the Materia!

The above in mind, Cure Materia (and other spells) will make Zack jump backwards before casting it, which may be enough to keep him out of harm's way and heal himself.

The Battle Stance, unlocked after Chapter 6, by default uses the attack and dodge buttons at once, but it's very easy to accidentally attack and kill an enemy you meant to hit with a standard attack. To avoid this, you can intentionally hold the dodge button first, then attack.

The Battle Stance can be prepared in advance if you hold down the two buttons during an existing action, like an attack animation or the Activating Combat Mode screen. This is very helpful in chaining multiple Battle Stance moves together without wasting much time (and pre-empting the accidental attack issue described in the previous tip).

Equipment Tips

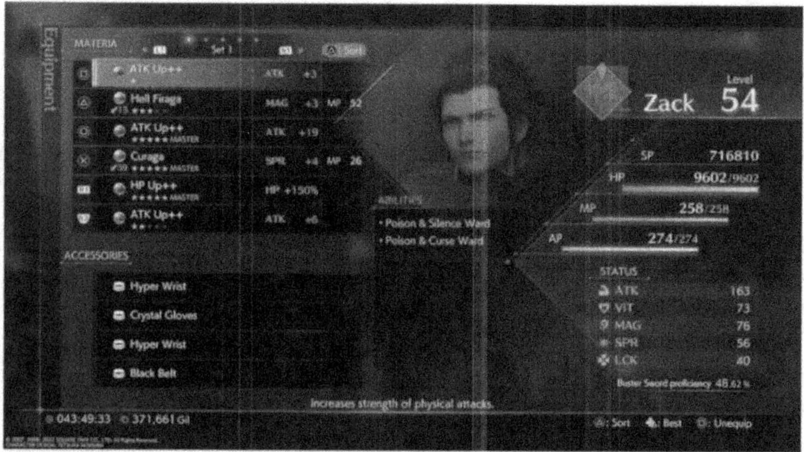

Swap Materia out regularly. Materia can be upgraded by the DMW to a maximum level of 5 Stars, where they're at their strongest. Try and swap in new Materia after one has reached 5 Stars: not only will this increase your viable options, but they will have more powerful effects when you use them in Materia Fusion.

Yellow Command Materia have increased damage if performed in the middle of Zack's 5-hit combo. For this reason, try striking four times with the combo, then using the Ability for maximum damage!

Use Materia Fusion! You regularly get lots of Materia from Chests for this reason, and knowing the right recipes can get you access to powerful Materia far earlier than buying them or finding them in a Chest first. You don't have to fuse anything either: the game will tell you what your combination will make, giving you plenty of space to experiment and see what you can make.

Accessories can really help you out in a number of ways, including boosting Zack's stats, and providing immunity to certain status ailments like Poison and Silence. Make sure you equip them to either boost your play style, or compensates for your weaknesses.

DMW - Digital Mind Wave Tips

While the DMW isn't completely random, you still cannot rely on it as a method of getting out of a jam (say, relying on a Summon, since you can't manually trigger successful rolls). With that in mind, you should prepare for battles as if you have no DMW at all, and treat anything you get from it as bonuses.

That being said, lengthy boss battles are a possible exception, since they last so long that you'll probably get certain DMW results eventually. As well, late in the game you'll be able to buy Materia that increases the likelihood of rolling specific characters.

Unlike the PSP original, Limit Breaks and Summons have to be triggered manually. This allows some strategy so that you can use them when you need it (especially important for Healing Wave).

However, Zack can only have ONE Limit Break and/or Summon on call at once. If the DMW successfully rolls another Limit Break or Summon, it will replace whatever Zack has in reserve! So don't wait on them for TOO long.

Leveling up is completely obscured in Crisis Core, but despite being tied to the DMW, IT IS NOT RANDOM! Zack will still earn XP by defeating enemies, and once you have enough, the DMW will have a heavily weighted chance to line up three 7s and initiate it. You cannot get three 7s to appear in the DMW purely through waiting: you must have enough XP for it to happen first!

If you get two of the same characters on the DMW (indicated by a flash), you may want to wait and see if you'll get a Limit Break or Summon, which can really help during a fight.

Limit Breaks and Summons give SP used to spin the DMW (10 SP per spin): Limit Verges give hundreds of SP, while Summons give thousands!

If you happen to get a Limit Break that hits a single target, such as Octaslash, Murderous Thrust or 1000 Needles, it's important that you target the enemy you want to hit with it first! Otherwise Zack may hit an enemy you don't want him to.

Side Quest Mission Tips

Side quest Missions are the primary way for Zack to level up and prepare for future story Chapters. If you're finding certain story battles to be too tough, spend an hour playing these Missions to improve Zack's abilities and get new Materia and Accessories.

If you're not having any trouble in the story Chapters, you may want to consider saving side quest Missions until after you've completed Chapter 6. This is when Zack picks up the Battle Stance: the more you use it, the more perks you unlock. Thus, saving Missions until this point gives you plenty of space to unlock them!

When on optional Missions in Reunion, use spells like Cure instead of items like Potions. Your HP, MP and AP will be restored as soon as you finish the Mission, while Potions, Elixirs and Somas won't!

Make sure to fully explore optional Mission areas! Exploring away from the path leading straight to the objective Destination will often reward you with Chests, as well as simply more battles to get XP from.

Every so-often you'll unlock an optional Mission in the "M8: Zack the Materia Hunter" section. DO ALL OF THESE IMMEDIATELY. This will almost always lead to a Mission that has you add a new Summon to the DMW. Summons are incredibly powerful moves that can turn the tide of a fight or press your advantage, so you'll want to have as many as possible to make the most of your battles!

REUNION CHANGES TO THE PSP CRISIS CORE

General & New Features

This section covers the brand new features added to the game, as well as more general changes.

All cutscenes, cinematics and Limit Breaks can now be paused and/or skipped (Summons could be skipped even in the original version).

You can now Sprint by clicking the left stick. This makes certain parts of the game easier, such as the item collection minigames in Banora and the Sector 5 Slums.

Reunion has a new Target Lock feature, allowing the camera and/or Zack to always target a specific enemy. This is very useful for Limit Breaks that only hit a single opponent, such as Octaslash and Murderous Thrust.

The game now supports rumble, which was not present in the PSP version due to the system's lack of rumble motors. Rumble is used for combat impacts, as well as to assist timing in certain minigames, such as the Squatting minigame.

Subtitles are no longer permanently active, and can be turned off in the options menu. The exception are the more basic scenes with "text boxes" on the bottom, which are always displayed.

It's also possible to choose between the Japanese and English dialogue, even in the middle of the game. However the subtitles will only adhere to the English script.

You can now sort your Items and Materia by recently acquired and their level.

The Materia Fusion screen now displays what the final output Materia will be while selecting the second Materia. In the PSP version, you had to select the Fuse button first before you could see this.

After Zack talks to Director Lazard in Chapter 4, Results Bonuses are unlocked, which refills Zack's HP, MP and/or AP meters for performing well in an encounter (to a maximum of +100% for each). This can include blocking all damage, killing all enemies without getting hit, or landing killing blows with Magic, an Ability, a Limit Break or a Summon. These bonuses can stack, although the block damage and no damage rewards are mutually exclusive.

When Zack gains the Buster Sword, he can use the new Battle Stance. The Battle Stance allows Zack to use stronger attacks, prevents flinching during them, and lets him parry enemy attacks after blocking. Assuming the Battle Stance costs 10 AP.

Using the Battle Stance improves Zack's proficiency with the Buster Sword and unlocks new perks, such as stronger damage protection when Guarding, or the next attack being able to break the 9,999 damage limit.

The game now has an options menu accessible from the main and pause menus, allowing control over aspects such as:

Toggling the game difficulty without having to start a new playthrough.

Toggling Subtitles, Vibration and Destination Markers.

Swapping between the English and Japanese voice languages.

Auto-Advance dialogue, for scenes which normally ask you to press X to advance them.

A full suite of camera settings, including camera distance and behavior.

Sound and brightness settings.

Limited button customization.

Presentation and Story

This section covers changes regarding the graphical and audio presentation of Crisis Core, as well as notable story changes.

Most obviously, the game has been completely remade graphically in Unreal Engine 4, the same engine used for Final Fantasy VII Remake. This gives many areas of the game a much higher level of fidelity, and certain regions now bear greater resemblance to their appearance in VII Remake.

While not as graphically lavish as Remake, Reunion often has parity by way of shared assets, lighting and rendering techniques. This gives it a much glossier, high-contrast look compared to the PSP original.

Similar to the above, the UI has been completely redesigned to match the aesthetic seen in Final Fantasy VII: Remake.

All cutscenes now use one single, high-quality model for all characters. In the PSP version, cutscenes would often use models with a simpler head with an animated texture representing the mouth. These were typically ones where dialogue was represented as text boxes on the bottom of the screen.

While the FMV cinematics have not been remade; they use higher resolution videos than the PSP original did. This can sometimes conflict with any revised Reunion designs, such as the grip of Zack's SOLDIER sword.

The design of the Buster Sword's cross-guard, grip and pommel has been changed to the one used in the original Final Fantasy VII and its remake. This includes Crisis Core's old FMV cinematics, where it has been composited in. The original PSP version used a more ornate, golden hilt design with a red grip inherited from the Advent Children movie.

The PSP version had many cinematics that were FMVs of in-engine footage. While they're still FMVs in Reunion, they're footage of the scenes presented in Reunion's Unreal Engine 4 engine.

The FMV cinematics for the Summons have been completely remade.

The script has been completely retranslated, resulting in many instances of characters saying the same things with different words, or completely different things from before.

The entire game has been given a brand new sound mix, including the FMV cinematics inherited from the PSP version.

Voiced dialogue is now present throughout the entire game, including basic scenes with permanent subtitles on the bottom, and the DMW flashback scenes. This results in a great many characters having more voice lines, such as Kunsel, or having a voice at all!

The English audio uses the modern cast rather than their original ones, which results in parity with Final Fantasy VII Remake. All VO has been re-recorded, even for characters who share the same voice actors between both versions.

The soundtrack has been rescored by Takeharu Ishimoto, the composer for the original PSP version. It follows the template set by the 2007 Crisis Core, but is still different, having a subtler feel.

The post-credits FMV cinematic, which recreates the opening of Final Fantasy VII, has been changed:

The Aerith section has been reconstructed using footage from Final Fantasy VII: Remake's intro. This is edited to be more authentic to the original Final Fantasy VII's opening, however the layout of LOVELESS Avenue conflicts with Crisis Core.

The ending with Cloud on the train is the original Crisis Core cinematic, to show Cloud bowing into the Buster Sword as Angeal and Zack did before him.

Controls and Camera

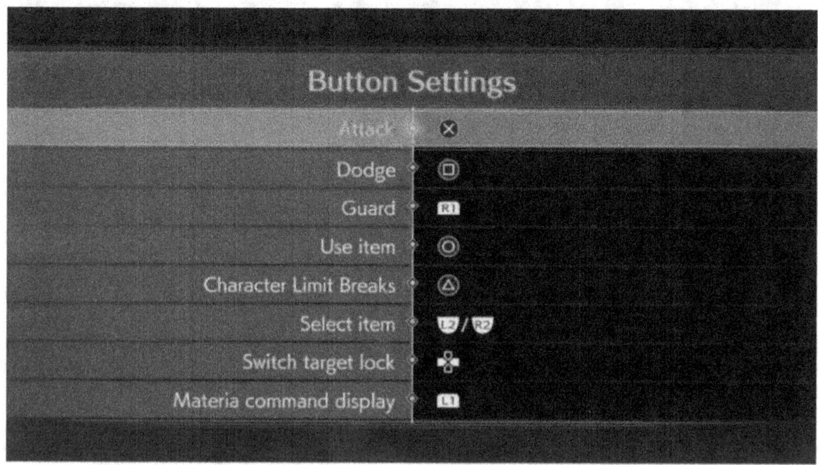

Thanks to Reunion releasing on platforms with more buttons than the PSP had, we have this section describing the changes made to the controls and camera behavior.

Camera controls are mapped to the right analog stick by default rather than the bumpers, allowing for vertical movement and moving the camera at slower speeds.

Because of the above, you can now rotate the camera during combat. Because L and R were used for combat functions in the 2007 Crisis Core, the camera couldn't be controlled, so it tried to fit all enemies on screen at once.

The camera no longer stops if it makes contact with a wall or other object. It will now move closer to Zack as it keeps rotating, then slide back to its normal distance once it has the space. This makes it much more usable in tight spaces, such as in the side-quest Missions.

If Zack isn't at full HP while outside combat, the player can now press Up on the D-Pad to instantly replenish Zack's health using available healing items. Lower items are always prioritized first (so if you have 5 Potions and an X-Potion, the normal Potions will be used up first).

If Zack has any unread mail, you can now press the right bumper to jump straight to the Mail Box's Inbox.

Similarly, while on a side quest Mission you can jump straight to the Missions menu with a button prompt.

Combat

This section covers the changes made to modernize and improve Crisis Core's combat.

Reunion generally has easier, more forgiving combat compared to the PSP version. This makes it more viable to mainline the story Chapters without doing a lot of the optional Missions to keep up.

Zack has faster and more fluid combat animations that make him more versatile and nimble on the battlefield. His sword combo is performed more quickly, he runs at a faster speed, dashes to Target Locked enemies rather than running, and recovers from the Evade Roll sooner.

At the same time, enemy AI is also faster and more responsive to Zack's actions to compensate, meaning it's still tricky to get Critical Hits by attacking them from behind.

You can now escape from non-mandatory random encounters. Run Zack into the encounter's barrier for a few seconds, and he'll be able to escape.

The use of Materia and the Sword has been reworked: each Materia is assigned to a different button combination, while Attack remains on X (or the Xbox / Nintendo equivalent). This makes better use of the buttons that weren't available on PSP, meaning the player can quickly use the function they need.

In the original PSP version, all of these were tied to a menu similar to Minecraft's Inventory hotbar, and the player had to use the L and R buttons to scroll over to what they needed, sacrificing the ability to attack with the sword all the while.

The original "Materia bar" from the PSP version now houses common items, including Potions, Elixirs and Phoenix Downs, and navigated using the triggers rather than the bumpers. In the PSP version, you have to scroll to an Items icon before you could do this.

It's now possible to Guard (block) attacks with the right bumper. This will only reduce the damage of attacks in front of Zack, and he cannot move or turn while Guarding.

Zack no longer runs to the enemy by default when using a melee attack: instead he'll swing where he stands, even if it won't hit anything. The PSP functionality can be restored by using Target Lock, where Zack will dash to the target first before swinging.

Status ailments no longer persist between battles, and are now cleared after a fight is over.

Bosses and enemies now always display their stats as a label floating above them, including health meters, names, current status and elemental weaknesses. In the PSP version, you had to equip a Libra Materia first, and this information was displayed in the upper-right corner of the screen.

Bosses now power up their Limit Breaks via a Skill Power meter, during which they stop attacking. Dealing damage to them during this period will reduce the damage of their Limit Break, or prevent it entirely if you fully deplete their Skill Power meter.

DMW - Digital Mind Wave

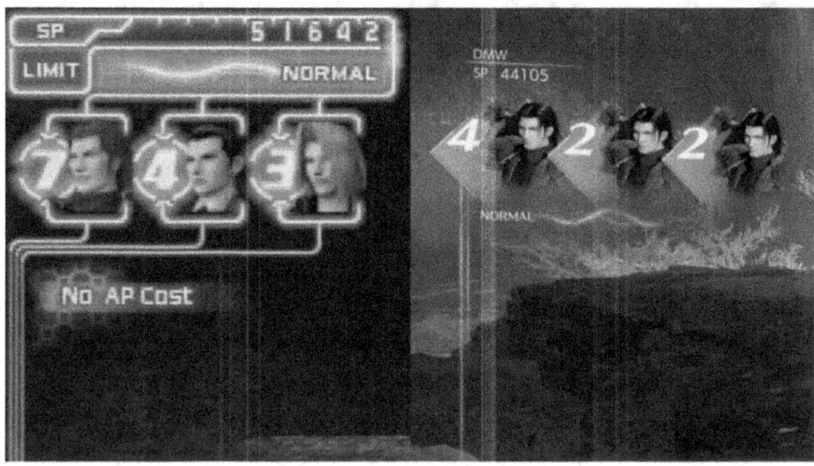

The DMW was a contentious feature in the original Crisis Core, hence there have been several changes made to how it works so that it fits into the gameplay more naturally.

The DMW's Modulating Phase, Summon Mode and Chocobo Mode no longer pause the game and take up the entire screen: they will now occur in the top-left corner while the player continues fighting normally. This also applies to the "flashback slides" of still images from FMV cinematics.

Because of the above change, this presentation of the DMW in the final battle is manually recreated with FMV cinematics.

Limit Breaks no longer trigger immediately after a successful DMW roll, and must now be triggered manually with a button prompt. This allows them to be used more strategically, such as with the Healing Wave Limit Break that fully heals Zack and grants a period of invincibility.

However, the prompt for a Limit Break or Summon will only last for the current battle. Once it's over, it disappears and will not be retained for the next fight.

Further, rolling a second Limit Break / Summon will replace the one currently held in reserve.

If the DMW is about to roll a set of numbers that levels up either Zack or his Materia, but the fight ends before the roll is completed, they will now be leveled up anyway. In the PSP version, you had to get a "completed" roll to get a level up.

Viewing a memory flashback video for a character in the DMW no longer guarantees a successful roll of that character after the video has finished.

Saving

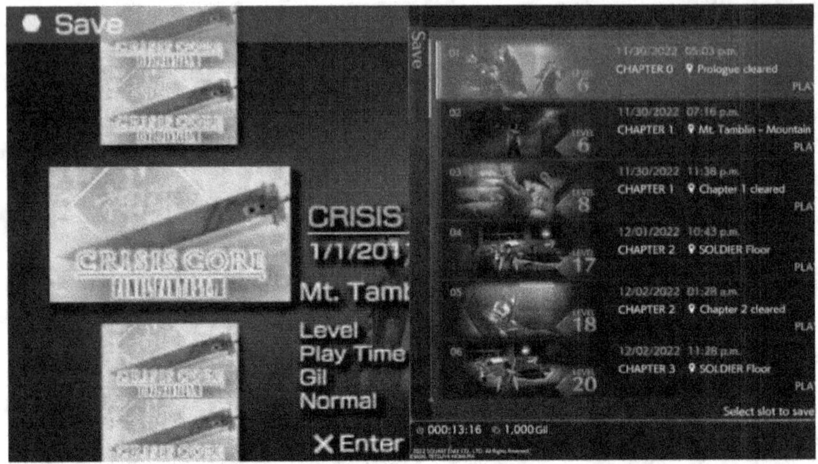

This section covers the changes made to how the game handles saving, as well as the Save Points themselves.

The game now has an Autosave feature that saves your progress automatically. There is only one Autosave slot.

Save Points now automatically restore Zack's HP, MP and AP for free when he touches them. In the original PSP version, the only way to do this was to enter a Mission other than "Shinra's Basic Training" and then exit it.

While this may look like it circumvents the Potion Promotion lady in the lobby of the Shinra Building, she is still very useful in getting the Raise buff (aka a free revive after death).

Loading a save can now be done at any time via the Pause Menu, even when not at a Save Point. In the 2007 version, you had to restart the game entirely to return to the title screen's Load function.

You are now limited to 30 save slots (plus one Autosave file), rather than as many as you have space for like on PSP.

When standing at a Save Point, you can now jump directly to the Missions screen with a button prompt. This replaces the "Delete" shortcut from the PSP version.

Side Quest Missions

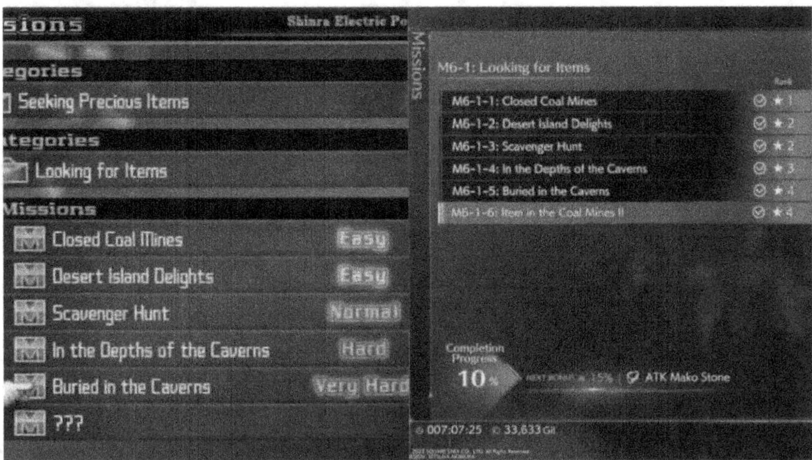

Side Quest Missions, the ones accessible at Save Points, have also had various changes made to them.

Missions are now graded using a Star system that remains static throughout the entire game. In the original PSP version, they were graded using words (Very Easy, Easy, Normal, Hard and Very Hard) which adjusted according to Zack's current level.

Missions will now display their completion rewards, as well as how many Chests they have in them and how many of them you've found.

The rewards for hitting overall Mission completion milestones can now be viewed from a dedicated menu screen.

Missions can now be sorted according to All, New, Uncleared and Unopened Chests.

You'll now be notified of new Missions as soon as they're unlocked, rather than when you reach a Save Point. This is particularly helpful for Mission lines you can only unlock by talking to people around Midgar.

Further, after clearing a Mission or series of Missions given to you by a specific individual, you're told to report back to them after you've completed them.

Missions now have Destination icons to mark where you should go to complete them. These can be turned off in the Options menu to veer closer to the PSP version.

The trigger zones for random encounters in Missions are slightly smaller than before, making it easier to run around and avoid them.

The encounter rate in the wide open field Mission areas has been reduced.

Mission encounter areas no longer trigger a second time after collecting a nearby Chest. You must now leave the area via one of the exits in order for this to happen.

Rewards from Mission Chests are now only kept if you then successfully complete the Mission. If you open any Chests and then abort, you no longer keep their rewards!

Miscellaneous

This section lists changes that don't fit into any of the previous categories, or are considered very minor.

The intro movie and title screen have been separated. In the PSP version, the New / Load Game options would be overlaid over the intro movie, with the "title screen" not appearing until it was over.

The title screen has been expanded, letting you customize your options, Continue from the most recent Save / Autosave, and for the PS5 version, convert save data from the PS4 version of the game to the PS5 version.

Further, it's now possible to quit back to the title screen from the pause menu, a function not available in the original game.

There is no longer a fade to black between the Briefing Room's supply pod area and the main conference room.

A few extra Chests have been placed throughout various levels, while others have been moved slightly and/or had their rewards changed.

The public Midgar areas, such as the Sector 8 Fountains and the Sector 5 Slums, are now populated with additional NPCs, although they cannot be talked to.

The Shinra Model sA-37 in the Exhibit Room no longer has the Midgar's Motor Group logo on it, likely because it looks like the Harley Davidson Motorcycles logo.

The industrial Mission zones now have much greater draw distances.

The wide-open field areas now have red diamonds to mark the level boundaries, similar to other levels in the game (although touching them does not give the Leave Mission prompt).

Thanks to the graphical upgrades, the photos of Angeal in his mother's house correctly match Zack's descriptions of them, rather than being blurry and ambiguous like the PSP version.

The little girl in the Sector 5 Slums no longer comments about an overly pleasant treatment she got from her "don" uncle (an allusion to Don Corleone from the original game), likely due to the suggestion that Don is a pedophile.

The Random Encounter trick in the Alert Head Sniper Rifle minigame has been adjusted: the first random encounter on the path has been removed. This means you must use the third Sniper Rifle before you have the two encounter spots needed to grind out KILL Points and fully upgrade the gun.

The rewards for performing well in the Alert Head Sniper Rifle minigame are now given automatically, rather than from Chests. This prevents the player from accidentally missing them by heading West at the Save Point, which concludes the level.

The number of Chests in the Gongaga waterfall minigame has been reduced from 11 to 10. 10 is still enough Chests to collect the full reward at the end, but it means the player must perform a perfect run of the minigame to get all of its rewards.

Non-Changes

This last section deals with surprising facets of the game that were not changed from the PSP version.

There is still no Chapter Select or cutscene viewer. This means that more than half of the Trophies in the game are permanently missable if you don't make full use of the save slots.

Almost all loading screen and transition points have been retained, despite the more powerful hardware. For example, there is still a loading transition from the Sector 8 plaza to LOVELESS Avenue.

While the Summon FMVs have been remade, the other story-based cinematics are the same ones used in the PSP version of the game. This can conflict occasionally with the designs and art style used for Reunion.

After gaining the Buster Sword, Zack still strikes using the sharp edge. In a later cutscene, he claims to only attack with the blunt edge to reduce wear, tear and rust, but this still only applies to cutscenes.

The SOLDIER outfit Cloud wears towards the end of the game is still the standard SOLDIER 1st Class outfit. While this retains continuity with the FMV cinematics from the original Crisis Core, it conflicts with the more industrial design seen in Crisis Core's post-credits scene, the original Final Fantasy VII, and its Remake.

HOW TOS

How to Get All Summons

Summons are incredibly powerful moves that can turn the tide of battle, or assist in pressing your advantage. However, all of them are completely optional, meaning it's possible to go through the entire game without acquiring one!

There are two types of Summon in the game: "Boss" Summons, which appear in the DMW's Summon Mode, and "Mascot" Summons, who appear in the DMW's Chocobo Mode. These are considered different from Limit Breaks, who are the various human characters Zack meets throughout the story: you'll acquire these automatically and have filled them all out by the time you finish Chapter 6.

How to Get All Boss Summons

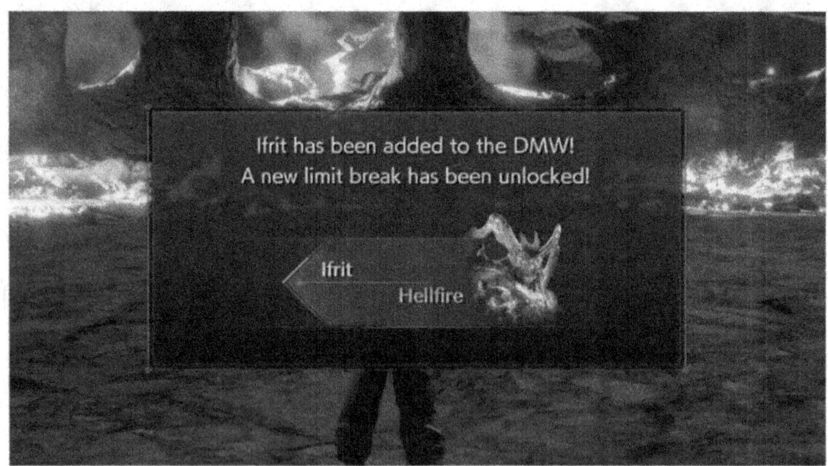

Each of the "Boss" Summons is fought at least once in the story, but acquiring them for your personal use typically requires completing a side quest Mission where you have to fight the Summon a second time with an expanded moveset (but there are exceptions).

Ifrit: After fighting Ifrit in Wutai, you'll unlock Mission M1-1-1: Rematch with Ifrit.

Bahamut: After fighting Bahamut in Banora, you'll unlock Mission M8-1-3: Clash with Genesis Troops. Beat that to unlock M8-1-4: Rematch with Bahamut.

Odin: Continue the M8-1 Mission line described above and complete M8-1-6: Mystery Materia.

Phoenix: Begin Chapter 9 and start the Seven Wonders side quest by talking to the boy. Then, find the Materia at the base of the water tower.

Bahamut Fury: Find this Summon's Materia in the North-West area of Mission M8-5-6, the final Mission with Yuffie. This series starts with M8-4-1: Suspicious Mail 1 unlocked part-way through Chapter 4, but will get very difficult for that point in the game.

How to Get All Mascot Summons

The "Mascot" Summons require either completing a side quest Mission or finding them in a chest one of these Missions.

Tonberry: Reach Chapter 3, then defeat the Tonberry in the East of M6-1-5: Buried in the Caverns. This will unlock the M10-2 Missions, the last of which will unlock Tonberry.

Magic Pot: Encounter during M10-2-3: Master Tonberry, then appease by performing Jump, Fira, Gravity and then Assault Twister. It can be found in other Missions too (M2-2-6, M2-5-4, M2-5-5, M2-5-6 and M7-6-6), but this is the earliest one.

Chocobo: Complete Mission M8-4-1: Suspicious Mail 1, which unlocks part-way through Chapter 4.

Cait Sith: Complete Mission M8-4-3: Suspicious Mail 3.

Moogle: Complete Mission M8-4-4: Suspicious Mail 4.

Cactuar: Reach Chapter 5 and defeat the Kactuar in the North part of M3-1-3: Eliminate the Copies. This will unlock the M10-1 Missions, the last of which will unlock Cactuar.

How to Achieve 100% Sync With All Summons

Of course, once you've gotten a Summon, you may be interested in achieving 100% sync with them. This is actually very simple: just use the Summon once and you'll have 100% sync!

However, Summons have a lower likelihood of appearing than Limit Breaks do, especially the "Mascot" Summons that rely on the Chocobo Mode. They can be made more likely to appear by unlocking two specific stores, however that requires entering some very challenging Missions that you cannot feasibly complete until towards the end of the game.

For "Boss" Summons, unlock the Bone Village Commerce store by finding a Chest in Mission M7-5-3: Girl on the Desert Island, in the North-West corner of the map. These can alternatively be given as rewards for completing the M9-5 Mission line (M9 Missions are unlocked by completing the M8-5 Mission line with Yuffie).

For "Mascot" Summons, unlock the Junon Souvenirs store by finding a specific Chest in Mission M2-4-1: A Solitary Island, on the Eastern side of the map. The 1,000 Needles (Cactuar) and Murderous Thrust (Tonberry) Materia are also given as rewards for completing M9-4-3: A Fresh Start and M9-4-5: Only for SOLDIER, respectively.

How to Use the Battle Stance

How to Enter the Battle Stance

To enter the Battle Stance, hold down both the Attack and Dodge buttons at the same time.

Assuming the Battle Stance uses up a bit of AP, but fortunately, AP should be readily available to you unless you use Abilities (yellow Materia) a lot in your playstyle.

Once Zack has assumed the Battle Stance, he can then launch into several new moves.

While in the Battle Stance, Zack will block all incoming attacks ahead of him.

Zack will exit the Battle Stance after three seconds of inaction.

Here's a couple of extra tips to help with using the Battle Stance:

You can manually exit the Battle Stance with a dodge roll.

Zack will be completely immune to flinching while using Battle Stance techniques. This means that taking damage won't interrupt and stop his actions!

When holding down dodge and attack, it's very easy to accidentally attack and kill an enemy you meant to hit with a Battle Stance move. To avoid this, you can intentionally hold the dodge button first, then attack.

The Battle Stance can be prepared in advance if you hold down the two buttons during an existing action, like an attack or the Activating Combat Mode screen. This is very helpful in chaining multiple Battle Stance moves together without wasting much time (and pre-empting the accidental attack issue described earlier).

How Buster Sword Proficiency Works

Buster Sword Proficiency is an additional aspect to the Battle Stance. Here's what you need to know about how it works:

The Buster Sword Proficiency meter fills when Zack kills an enemy with a Battle Stance move, or when blocking damage in the initial Battle Stance pose.

Since the meter only fills when the enemy is killed, a good strategy is to deplete the enemy's health enough so that a Battle Stance technique will kill them.

A good technique is to wait for an enemy to prepare an attack, block in the Battle Stance pose, then immediately attack afterwards. This maximizes the amount you can fill the Proficiency meter by blocking and then attacking.

The meter is filled the same amount no matter the strength of the enemy.

Kills MUST be done using a Battle Stance technique. Standard attacks won't do anything.

There is an "enemy cap" of 10 for the number of kills in a single encounter that adds to the Proficiency meter. After the tenth kill, the meter is no longer added to.

In the side quest Missions, the kill cap of 10 extends to the entirety of the Mission! This means you cannot grind something like the 1,000 Shinra Troopers Mission to get to 100%.

As Zack increases his Buster Sword Proficiency, he'll unlock new perks and skills, some of which benefit ALL his melee combat, not just the Battle Stance. These are detailed in the next section below.

Your Buster Sword Proficiency progress is carried over into New Game +. However since Zack doesn't start the game with the Buster Sword, you cannot resume contributing to it until you complete Chapter 6 again.

Because it can take a long time to complete Buster Sword Proficiency, we recommend saving as many Missions as you can until after Chapter 6. This allows you to play through the Missions (many of which should be quite easy) and unlock many of the perks listed below.

All Battle Stance and Proficiency Abilities

The table below logs all of the abilities and skills you can unlock with the Battle Stance by increasing Zack's Buster Sword proficiency.

This table is incomplete, as we have yet to accomplish 100% proficiency.

Name	Unlocks at	Description
Strong Attack	0%	Press the Attack button after assuming the Battle Stance to strike once with a sweeping swing, then a second time with a VERY powerful downwards strike. Zack will charge at the enemy no matter the distance and even turn to face them mid-swing, but if they die, he will not face a new target. The attack can hit multiple enemies if others happen to be standing behind the target.
Enhanced Guard	0%	Zack's Guard now reduces damage by 80% (including while in the Battle Stance).
Necrosmose	0%	Zack regains a little bit of MP and AP every time he defeats an enemy, even outside the Battle Stance.
Damage Limit Break	23%	Any attack or Yellow Command Materia performed from the Battle Stance can break the 9,999 damage cap without the use of Brutal, the Genji Glove or Heike Soul. This is incredibly useful for making the most out of the Strong Attack's second strike, particularly on stronger bosses.
Barrier Piercing	47%	Any attack or Yellow Command Materia performed from the Battle Stance now ignores Barrier effects when dealing damage.

How to Get Costly Punch

Costly Punch is widely considered to be the best move in Crisis Core. While it has 38 base damage, this amount increases the more HP you have (with the slight exception of HP Breaks), meaning it can easily exceed 99,999 damage.

How Costly Punch Works

Here's how Costly Punch works in battle:

It has 38 base damage and ignores the target's Vitality, but takes a moment for Zack to actually throw the punch.

Further, Costly Punch will consume some HP with each use.

Costly Punch's damage is increased based on Zack's HP: the higher it is, the more powerful Costly Punch becomes. This allows it to easily reach the 99,999 damage cap.

However, if Zack's HP has the Break effect and is higher than its base amount (say, 3100/3000 HP), Costly Punch will do 0 damage.

How to Get the Genji Glove

While the Costly Punch can easily deal 99,999 damage, Zack starts out the game with a damage cap of 9,999, meaning that by default he can only use Costly Punch at 1/10th of its potential strength, making it practically useless for endgame use.

Equipping the Genji Glove will raise Zack's damage cap to 99,999 (and make all attacks Critical Hits), making Costly Punch live up to its reputation.

To get the Genji Glove, go to Mission M9-4-6: Biomechanical Threats (the M9 Mission section is unlocked after clearing M8-5-6: Treasure Info 6). There, head for the large room West of the starting point to find it on the Western corner of the room.

How to Find Costly Punch

While most players will prefer to craft Costly Punch using Materia Fusion, it is possible to simply find Costly Punch directly. You can do that using one of the following two methods:

Complete 55% of the Side-Quest Missions.

50% Rare Steal chance from Mako Ifrit in M9-5-1: Hojo's Monsters.

Find in M9-5-4: Abnormal Power in the South-East corner of the map.

How to Craft Costly Punch

Most players will typically prefer to craft Costly Punch rather than find it, since this can be done far earlier. This is done by using one of the other four "Punch" Accessories, and a "DMW Materia" (which are Materia you can buy that increases the likelihood for a specific Limit Break or Summon to appear in the DMW).

First, here's where you can get the "DMW Materia":

Unlock the Junon Souvenirs store by finding a specific Chest in Mission M2-4-1: A Solitary Island, on the Eastern side of the map. Here you can buy Materia for "Mascot" Summons like Chocobo and Moogle.

Unlock the Bone Village Commerce store by finding a Chest in Mission M7-5-3: Girl on the Desert Island, in the North-West corner of the map. Here you can buy Materia for "Boss" Summons like Bahamut and Ifrit for 10,000 gil each.

These can alternatively be given as rewards for completing Missions in the M9-4 and M9-5 Mission lines. M9 Missions are unlocked by completing the M8-5 Mission line with Yuffie.

The second ingredient that you'll need is one of the four "Punch" Accessories that aren't Costly Punch itself. These are Goblin Punch, Iron Fist, Magical Punch or Hammer Punch.

Because Iron Fist, Magical Punch and Hammer Punch can only be crafted using a Goblin Punch anyway, most players don't bother with them and just get Goblin Punch, especially since Goblin Punch can be found much earlier than the other three.

With the above in mind, here's how to directly find all five "Punch" Accessories that you can use to craft a Costly Punch:

Goblin Punch:

- Collect 10 Chests in the Gongaga Waterfall minigame in Chapter 10.

- 50% Steal chance from Vajradhara Kumbhira in M4-4-4: Wutai in the Slums, M4-4-5: Anti-Shinra Base or M9-2-1: The Third Power.

- Find in M7-5-1: Boy in the Caverns, in the middle of the Western maze.

- Clear M9-2-5: To the Lower Levels.

Iron Fist:

- Steal from a G General in M3-4-3: Reinforced Copies or M3-4-4: Return to Midgar.

Magical Punch:

- Rare Steal from a G General in M3-4-3: Reinforced Copies or M3-4-4: Return to Midgar.

- Clear M4-5-6: Wutai Suppression.

- Clear M5-4-2: Experiment No. 120.

- Find in M6-5-5: Arms Development Dept. at the Northern edge of the map.

- Find in M7-5-5: Twins in the Caverns, in the Southern part of the map.

- Clear M9-3-4: Genesis's Super Weapon.

    Hammer Punch:

    - Find in M3-5-1: Genesis's Forces on the Southern edge of the map.

    - 50% Steal chance from Vajradhara Kinnara in M4-4-6: Anti-SOLDIER Weapons and M9-2-1: The Third Power

    - Clear M9-3-1: To the End.

- Once you've gotten your ingredients, add them to Materia Crafting (this will cost around 12,000 SP):

- 1 Goblin Punch / Iron First / Magical Punch / Hammer Punch

- 1 DMW Materia

Refining Costly Punch

Whatever method you've used to acquire Costly Punch, you can make it even better by combining it with various crafting materials using Materia Fusion.

- Add the Costly Punch.

- Add the Hellfire Materia.

- In the Item slot, add Phoenix Downs.

Your final output will be a Costly Punch with +999% HP. This is just a starting point!

Next, add Costly Punch and another Hellfire Materia into the Materia slots.

Now you'll be adding a Materia Fusion item to give Costly Punch a different perk, one focused on boosting one of Zack's core stats. Because Costly Punch has +999% HP, you'll only have to give it one of these Fusion items in order to give it the maximum boost of +100.

Use the list below to choose the material corresponding to the stat you want to boost:

- +100 ATK: Hero Drink

- +100 VIT: Adamantite

- +100 MAG: Dark Matter

- +100 SPR: Mythril

- +100 LCK: Gyshal Greens

- +999 HP: Fat Chocobo Feather

- +999 MP: Lunar Harp

- +999 AP: Zeio Nut

How to Get the Genji Armor Set

How to Get the Genji Armor

The Genji Armor is considered to be the ultimate health-based equipment, thanks to several buffs: Break HP Limit (which raises the HP cap from 9,999 to 99,999), Auto-Endure (meaning Zack's moves will never be interrupted), and Auto-Regen, meaning Zack's HP will slowly refill over time.

However, the core Genji Armor is easily the most irritating of the four to get, because you need to have reached 100% progress on all Limit Breaks and Summons (which of course means you'll need to acquire all the Summons as well).

Once you've achieved 100% sync with all DMW images, you'll also have to go to the DMW screen from the pause menu to unlock the Genji Armor.

The following two sub-sections will go over how to get all the Limit Breaks and Summons, and how to achieve 100% sync for all of them.

How to 100% all DMW Limit Breaks

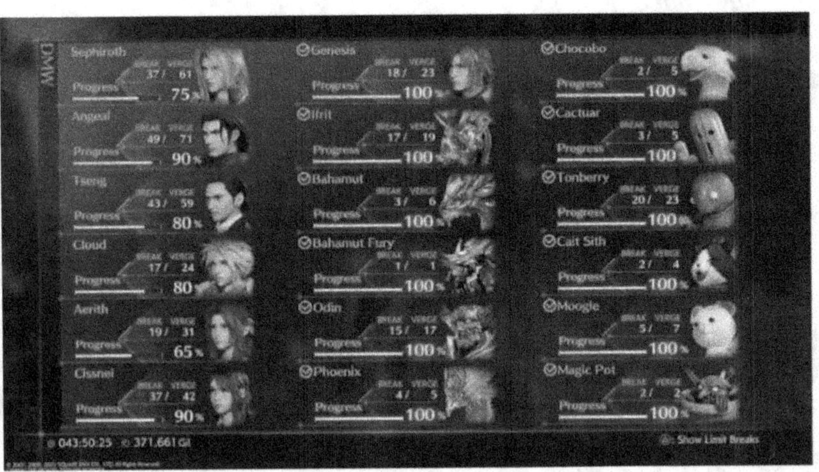

The DMW Limit Breaks are the specific characters that Zack meets throughout the story, such as Angeal and Sephiroth.

The Limit Breaks are the simplest to get but the hardest to fill out. You'll have acquired them all by the time you complete Chapter 6 in Modeoheim.

To achieve 100% sync, you'll need to have seen all of the memory scene videos associated with them.

It's well worth pointing out that several DMW scenes are inaccessible for story reasons because they haven't happened yet. You'll have full access to them once you reach Chapter 10.

You can increase the likelihood of a specific character lining up on the DMW by buying their Materia from the Research Dep. QMC+ store:

You can unlock this store by finding it in a Chest after meeting Cissnei in Gongaga Village.

Since Gongaga is a story mission, it can be permanently missed!

Once you've unlocked the store, each Limit Break Materia will cost 10,000 gil.

At first the Materia will increase the likelihood by 5x, but leveling them up will increase it to 9x. This can be increased even more by having multiple Limit Break Materia equipped.

If you want to level up your Materia faster, unlock the Junon Souvenirs shop by going to Mission 2-4-1: A Solitary Island and opening the Chest on the Eastern side of the map.

How to 100% all DMW Summons

The DMW Summons are the various beasts Zack can call onto the battlefield. We've grouped them into two categories: "Boss" Summons like Ifrit and Bahamut, and "Mascot" Summons like Chocobo and Cactuar.

With DMW Summons, the hard part is acquiring the Summon: acquiring 100% sync for a Summon only requires you to use it once.

Each of the "Boss" Summons is fought at least once in the story, but acquiring them for your personal use typically requires completing a side quest Mission (but there are exceptions).

Ifrit: After fighting Ifrit in Wutai, you'll unlock Mission M1-1-1: Rematch with Ifrit.

Bahamut: After fighting him in Banora, you'll unlock Mission M8-1-3: Clash with Genesis Troops. Beat that to unlock M8-1-4: Rematch with Bahamut.

Odin: Continue the M8-1 Mission line and complete M8-1-6: Mystery Materia.

Phoenix: Begin Chapter 9 and start the Seven Wonders side quest by talking to the boy. Then, find the Materia at the base of the water tower.

Bahamut Fury: Find it in the North-West area of Mission M8-5-6, the final Mission with Yuffie. This series starts with M8-4-1: Suspicious Mail 1 unlocked part-way through Chapter 4, but will get very difficult for that point in the game.

The "Mascot" Summons require either completing a side quest Mission or finding them in one of these Missions.

Tonberry: Reach Chapter 3, then defeat the Tonberry in the East of M6-1-5: Buried in the Caverns. This will unlock the M10-2 Missions, the last of which will unlock Tonberry.

Magic Pot: Encounter during M10-2-3: Master Tonberry, then appease by performing Jump, Fira, Gravity and then Assault Twister. It can be found in other Missions too (M2-2-6, M2-5-4, M2-5-5, M2-5-6 and M7-6-6), but this is the earliest one.

Chocobo: Complete Mission M8-4-1: Suspicious Mail 1, which unlocks part-way through Chapter 4.

Cait Sith: Complete Mission M8-4-3: Suspicious Mail 3.

Moogle: Complete Mission M8-4-4: Suspicious Mail 4.

Cactuar: Reach Chapter 5 and defeat the Kactuar in the North part of M3-1-3: Eliminate the Copies. This will unlock the M10-1 Missions, the last of which will unlock Cactuar.

Once you've gotten the Summons you need, you can increase the likelihood of them appearing in the DMW by buying their Materia from a specific store for 10,000 gil. These will be named after the Summon's attack, NOT the name of the Summon themselves.

For "Boss" Summons, unlock the Bone Village Commerce store by finding a Chest in Mission M7-5-3: Girl on the Desert Island, in the North-West corner of the map. These can alternatively be given as rewards for completing the M9-5 Mission line (M9 Missions are unlocked by completing the M8-5 Mission line with Yuffie).

For "Mascot" Summons, unlock the Junon Souvenirs store by finding a specific Chest in Mission M2-4-1: A Solitary Island, on the Eastern side of the map. The 1,000 Needles (Cactuar) and Murderous Thrust (Tonberry) Materia are also given as rewards for completing M9-4-3: A Fresh Start and M9-4-5: Only for SOLDIER, respectively.

The Summon attack Materia will initially increase the likelihood of that Summon appearing by 5x. This can be increased by leveling up the Materia to increase it to a maximum of x9.

For this reason, you may want to consider always keeping the Moogle Power Materia equipped. This is because the Moogle Power Limit Break will fully upgrade all equipped Materia!

How to Get the Genji Glove

The Genji Glove is the ultimate offensive Accessory. With this equipped, Zack gets the Break Damage Limit Ability, which makes all his attacks Critical Hits, and raises his damage cap from 9,999 to 99,999. This makes the Genji Glove required to get the Genji Shield, since you need to perform a move that deals 99,999 damage (among other things) to acquire it.

To get the Genji Glove, go to Mission M9-4-6: Biomechanical Threats (the M9 Mission section is unlocked after clearing M8-5-6: Treasure Info 6). There, head for the large room West of the starting point to find it on the Western corner of the room.

How to Get the Genji Shield

The Genji Shield is the ultimate defensive Accessory: it provides Zack with a permanent Barrier and MBarrier that nullifies all physical and magic attacks, and prevents all negative Status ailments.

The Genji Shield is found by encountering a Magic Pot enemy in Mission M7-6-6: The Determined Recruiter. This is the final Mission of the Yuffie treasure-hunting series: while this series can be started as early as midway through Chapter 5, the difficulty will eventually turn overwhelming for almost all players, so this can only feasibly be attempted later.

The Magic Pot will always add itself as a Summon first if you don't already have it. If you don't have the Magic Pot Summon, you'll have to find it twice: once to add the Summon, and again for the Genji Shield!

The Magic Pot enemy looks like a purple goblin in a yellow pot, and is a rare spawn in enemy encounters. Once you encounter it, it will ask you to perform a series of specific moves, so it's best to prepare for this in advance. These moves are:

Gil Toss. This is the reward for completing Mission M4-4-4: Wutai in the Slums.

Costly Punch: This one can be given as a Mission reward, but it's actually easier to make:

First, find the Research Dept QMC+ item in Gongaga Village, in the area where you meet Cissnei (this is MISSABLE!). Once you have it, buy any DMW Materia.

Second, the Goblin Punch is a reward for the waterfall minigame, also in Gongaga.

Third, use Materia Fusing and put in the Goblin Punch and DMW Materia. This will give you Costly Punch!

Alternatively, you can Steal this from Mako Ifrit in M9-5-1: Hojo's Monsters, or find it in a Chest in M9-5-4.

Any attack that deals 99,999 damage. Zack's normal damage cap is 9,999: to increase it, you'll need to equip the Genji Glove, described above. Costly Punch itself can meet this requirement, so you can just use it a second time!

Octaslash, the Sephiroth Limit Break. You can increase the likelihood of this move appearing by equipping Octaslash Materia from the Research Dept QMC+ store, which you can unlock by finding a Chest in Gongaga village. This is easier in the Reunion remake because you can manually trigger Octaslash after a successful Sephiroth roll.

How to Get the Genji Helm

The Genji Helm is the ultimate accessory for Magic and Ability users. With it equipped, all Magic, Abilities and Commands will cose 0 MP and AP. On top of that, it also gives Zack the Libra effect, meaning he'll always be able to see the full stats of any enemy in the game.

To get the Genji Helm, you'll first need to unlock the Net Shop Shade store. This can be found in a Chest in Mission M9-5-4: Abnormal Power. Here, bring up the map and locate the three paths with red barriers on the Southern edge of the map: head for the middle one to find a Chest next to it, which will unlock Net Shop Shade.

While you're here, head for the red barrier in the South-East corner of the map for Costly Punch. This is the move you need to appease the Magic Pot that gives you the Genji Shield, and is also widely considered to be the best Ability in the game.

Once you've unlocked the Net Shop Shade store, you can buy the Genji Helm for a hefty 1,000,000 gil.

THE BEST EQUIPMENT IN CRISIS CORE

Genji Armor Set

The Genji Armor Set, otherwise known as Genji Equipment, is bar-none the most powerful set of accessories in the game (with the debatable exception of the Heike Soul, detailed below). However, they are also the absolute hardest to acquire, as they are all considered absolute endgame equipment.

Their powerful buffs include breaking the HP and damage limit from 9,999 to 99,999, Auto-Endure, Auto-Regen, Barrier and MBarrier, Libra, and 0 MP / AP costs.

Head to our dedicated Genji Armor Set page to learn how to get them all:

How to Get All Genji Items

The Best Accessories in Crisis Core

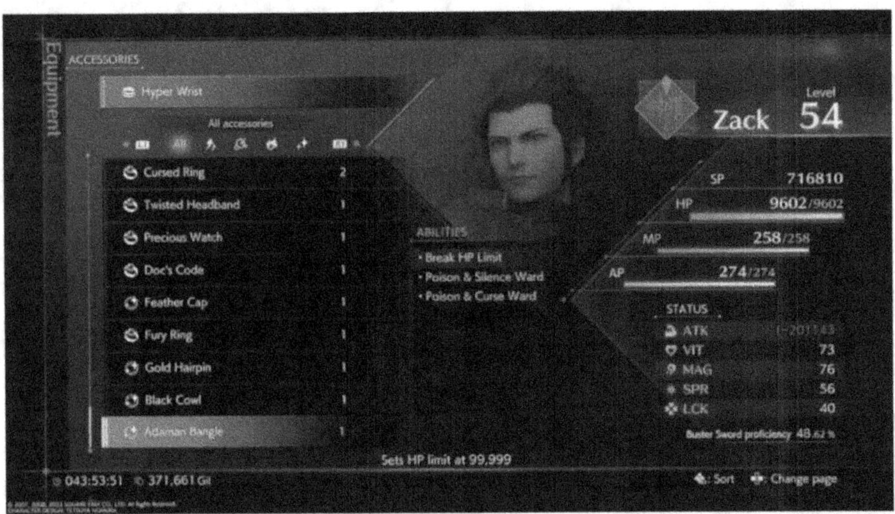

The table below details all of the best Accessories you can find in Crisis Core (with the exception of the Genji Armor, which has its own section). Many of these are designed to aid you in the harder Missions, and are not at all required to complete the story.

Armlets

Name	Effects	How to get
Dragon Armlet	Halves damage from Fire, Ice and Lightning attacks. +40% MP	Buy at Sec.7 Shop or Net Shop Duo for 20,000 gil.
Escort Guard	Nullifies Fire, Ice and Lightning attacks. +50% MP	Buy at Net Shop Duo for 40,000 gil.

Safety Bit	Prevents Instant Death +30 SPR	Find in Chest in M10-1-3: Cactuar Found? Complete the third Seven Wonders of Nibelheim mystery, the Wonder Bomb. Buy at Nibel Accessories for 5,000 gil
Wizard Bracelet	Absorbs Fire, Ice and Lightning attacks into HP. +60% MP	Clear M2-5-3: More Species Found Clear M7-5-6: Youngest in the Wasteland Buy at Sec.7 Shop or Network Shop Duo for 80,000 gil

Attack

Name	Effects	How to get
Element Blade	Adds Fire, Ice and Lightning to melee attacks. +50% MP +5 ATK and MAG	Find in M2-5-1: Investigation of the Caverns, ahead from the starting point. Clear M5-4-1: Experiment No. 119. Clear M9-2-3: Continuing in the Caves. Buy at Sec.7 Shop or Net Shop Duo for 20,000 gil.
Force of Nature	+100% Max MP +10 ATK, MAG, VIT and SPR Adds Fire, Ice and Lightning to Zack's melee attacks, and absorbs them from enemy attacks into HP.	Rare Steal from a G Enforcer in M3-5-4: Chase the Copies and M3-5-5: Defeat the Copies.

Ribbons

Name	Effects	How to get
Ribbon	Prevents all Status ailments, except Death	Steal from a Great Malboro in M2-5-6: The Great Beast or M6-6-5: The Melancholy Don. Clear M5-4-6: Experiment No. 124. Randomly-chosen item in a Level 5 Item Mugger, the Magic Pot Summon.
Super Ribbon	Prevents all Status ailments (including Death)	Clear M9-6-2: Lowest Tier. Steal from Malboro in M9-6-4: Biomechanical Threats

Rings

Name	Effects	How to get
Brigand's Gloves	Steals are always 100% successful.	Clear M7-4-2: Second Contact. Find in M9-3-5: Wutai's Best in the South-East corner of the map.

Doc's Code	A Potion is automatically consumed when Zack's HP falls below 25%.	Clear M6-2-5: Making Phoenix Down. Find in M9-5-2: Further Below, on the Northern edge of the map. Steal from Kactuare in M9-6-1: Toughest Monsters. Find and appease the Magic Pot in M10-2-3 with Jump, Fira, Gravity and Assault Twister.
Faerie Ring	Adds persistent Regen +20 SPR	Clear M7-6-2: A Recruiter's Close Call
Jeweled Ring	Doubles item and Materia drops from enemies +20 LCK	Encounter a Magic Pot in M2-5-4: New Cavern Found or M2-5-5: Another Cavern. Perform Ultima, Tri-Fire, Iron Fist and Electrocute. Find in M9-5-4: Abnormal Power in the Eastern side of the map. Buy at Net Shop Shade for 10,000 gil.
Mog's Amulet	Items dropped or Stolen from enemies are always rare +5 LCK	Clear M7-6-4: The Irritated Recruiter.
Moon Bracer	Adds persistent Barrier +10 SPR	Find in M1-5-4: Shinra Machines Unit on the Southern edge of the map. Clear M4-4-6: Anti-SOLDIER Weapons. Find in M9-4-3: A Fresh Start on the path that goes to the South-East corner of the map. Buy at Mythril Mine Trading for 10,000 gil (after clearing M2-4-5: Cave-In Investigation).
Precious Watch	Doubles gil looted from enemies +10 LCK	Clear M9-4-4: Machines Gone Haywire. Buy at Net Shop Shade for 10,000 gil.
Protect Ring	Adds persistent Barrier and MBarrier +20 SPR	Clear M7-6-3: A Recruiter in a Slump. Clear M9-3-2: Genesis's Challenge. Buy at Mythril Mine Trading for 30,000 gil (after clearing M2-4-5: Cave-In Investigation).
Shining Bracer	Adds persistent MBarrier. +10 SPR	Clear M6-4-5: Buried in the Plains. Find in M7-5-6: Youngest in the Wasteland, in the Western half of the map. Find in M7-6-5: The Frustrated Recruiter, in the North-Eastern part of the map. Find in M9-3-5: Wutai's Best, on the Western edge of the map. Find in M9-4-6: Only for 1st Class, in the North-Western part of the map. Buy at Mythril Mine Trading for 10,000 gil (after clearing M2-4-5: Cave-In Investigation).

Sniper Eye	All of Zack's attacks are Critical Hits	Find in M2-5-6: The Great Beast in the North-West corner of the map. Clear M9-4-6: Only for 1st Class. Buy at Network Shop Duo for 50,000 gil.

Special

Name	Effects	How to get
Adaman Bangle	HP cap raised to 99,999	Clear M7-3-6: P's Precognition Lv. 6. Find in M9-2-4: A New Path Discovered, on the Western edge of the map. Steal from the Grandpanzer in M9-3-3: Genesis's New Weapon. Find in M9-5-4: Abnormal Power, in the Eastern area of the map.
Black Cowl	AP cap raised to 9,999.	Find in M2-5-5: Another Cavern, in the North-West corner of the map. Clear M7-3-1: P's Precognition Lv. 1 Find in M9-3-3: Genesis's New Weapon, in the North-West corner of the map. Rare Steal from Diatryma in M9-6-4: Biomechanical Threat.
Brutal	Damage cap raised to 99,999.	Rare Steal from Crazy Sword in M3-5-4: Chase the Copies, M7-6-4: The Irritated Recruiter, and M9-4-1: Genesis's Ambition. Clear M7-4-6: Breakthrough. Clear M9-5-1: Hojo's Monsters. Find in M9-6-3: Weapons Gone Haywire, in the North-West corner of the map.
Dark Agent	Zero AP costs +50% HP & AP +100 ATK and VIT -50% AP -100 MAG & SPR	Find in M9-4-4: Machines Gone Haywire, in the North-East part of the map. Rare Steal from Mock Trooper A in M9-6-5: Life Form of Energy.
Divine Slayer	HP and Damage cap raised to 99,999 MP and AP cap raised to 9,999 +50 ATK, VIT, MAG, SPR and LCK. +100 HP, MP and AP.	Clear M9-6-6: The Reigning Deity by defeating Minerva.
Feather Cap	HP, MP and AP can Break up to 3x their normal amount.	Find in M4-3-2: Obliterate Advance Elements, in the North part of the map. Find and appease the Magic Pot in M10-2-3: Master Tonberry with Jump, Fira, Gravity and Assault Twister.

Gold Hairpin	MP cap raised to 9,999	Clear M7-3-4: P's Precognition Lv. 4. Find in M9-2-5: To the Lower Levels, at the end of the South-Eastern path.
Laurel Crown	Zero AP costs	Clear M9-5-4: Abnormal Power Find in M9-6-2: Lowest Tier, on the Northern edge of the map.
Magic Master	Zero MP costs +50% MP +100 MAG and SPR -50% HP and AP -100 ATK and VIT	Find in M9-4-5: Only for SOLDIER, on the side path to the East of the starting point. Rare Steal from Mock Trooper C in M9-6-5: Life Form of Energy.
Power Suit	+100% HP, +100 ATK and VIT -50% MP and AP -50 MAG and SPR	Find in M6-6-6: The Don's Twilight, in the South-East corner of the map. Clear M7-5-4: Second Son in the Wasteland Find in M7-6-3: A Recruiter in a Slump, in the South-West corner of the map. Steal from Vajradhara Asura in M9-3-5: Wutai's Best
Soul of Thamasa	Zero MP costs	Find in M9-4-4: Machines Gone Haywire, around the first bend of the stage. Find in 9-6-5: Life Form of Energy, in the Northern part of the map.
Ziedrich	Halves all incoming elemental damage +100 ATK, VIT, MAG and SPR	Find in M9-5-6: Even Deeper, in the South-West corner of the map.

PSP CHEATS

New Game++

To unlock a New Game++ option, beat the game with a New Game+ file and save after the ending and credits have concluded. You can then play through the game again with your items, gear, Materia, and more from your previous quest.

Sephiroth Foreshadowing

When you get to the part of the game where you have to assemble Aerith's flower cart, you should instead head back to the SOLDIER building and go to Lazard's office. Walk up to his desk, flip the camera around, and look at his computer screen. You'll see a picture of Sephiroth there, foreshadowing events to come.

Money Farming

A great way to get as much money as you want is by attempting the following. Once you acquire the spell called Quake, head to the Master Tonberry quest. Use Quake in every battle, which should deal the maximum 9,999 HP of damage while using 58 MP. An Ether costs 200 Gil, but a dead Tonberry is worth 500 Gil. You should therefore make a profit of 700-1,200 HP per battle. Repeat this process as much as you can to theoretically make as much money as you want.

Addition from dinamo_badblueboys:

Additionally, you can just kill the Tonberries on mission 10-2-3 and not have to use any MP, therefore saving any spent money. They only have 8,000-10,000 HP, and are easy to kill without Quake by the time you acquire that spell.

Genji Helm

You can acquire the Genji Helm in the Network Shop Shade, a shop that can be found on mission 9-5-4. It costs a million Gil, it equips No Cost MP and No Cost AP, and adds a permanent Libra affect.

Magic Pot DMW

When you encounter the rare and hard-to-find Magic Pots in the game, you're going to have to be well-prepared to fight them. That's because you need to attack them in a certain order with certain attack types, but the payout is worth it, because you'll net a Magic Pot DMW. An easy way to acquire this DMW is to head to Mission 10-2-3 (Master Tonberry) and find the Magic Pot there. Then, attack it in this order, and the DMW is yours: Fira, Gravity, Jump, Assault Twister.

Item Fusion Tome

To unlock the Item Fusion Tome, complete mission 7-2-1.

Correction from DJ JD

Conversation With Hojo

When you reach the Fusion Chamber and have a conversation with Hojo, he will ask you a series of questions. While there is no wrong answer to any question, the amount of SP you come out of the conversation with will actually depend on which answer you provide him. Below are the three questions he will ask you along with the SP point value of each possible answer.

When asked Which do you admire more?, answer Sephiroth for 300 SP or Angeal for 100 SP.

When asked What do you think Shinra needs most right now?, answer more SOLDIER operatives for 200 SP or more science and technology for 400 SP.

When asked Which do you believe to be more befitting a SOLDIER member?, answer a person who gives it all for 200 SP, or a person unafraid to challenge Shinra for 300 SP.

Rifle Fun in Nibel Plains

There comes a point late in the game where you're inserted into the Nibel Plains and are given a rifle to take out enemies from afar. There's a level-up system on the rifle that's explained before you kill the first enemy. While it seems that you can't possibly level up the rifle entirely before you reach the conclusion of Nibel Plains, you can actually backtrack at certain points to make enemies respawn. By doing so, you can accumulate seemingly-endless amounts of experience to be used on your rifle.

Shinra Manor Combo

At a certain point in the game, you will arrive with a very ill Cloud at Shinra Manor and will have to find new clothes for him. There are four rooms in the manor that you will find are locked as you explore, and if you look through the keyholes of the locked doors, you will see certain items that when counted will give you a combination to a safe which holds Vital Slash Materia. Here's how to find the digits (From the Editor: this submitter gave us a combination, but in fact the combination is randomly generated on each game, hence you'll have to find it on your own by doing the following).

First Digit - Knowledge Overflowing (In the room nearest Cloud, you will find a room full of bookshelves. Count the books on the shelves for this number.)

Second Digit - Unfamiliar Faces (In a room on the first floor you will find eerie apparitions floating in a room. Count them for this digit.)

Third Digit - Tasty Reminders From Home (The second locked room on the second floor will hold dumbapples and cans of juice. Count them.)

Fourth Digit - On All Four Legs (The other locked room on the first floor holds a bunch of chairs. Count them up for the final number.)

Genji Shield

The Genji Shield is an extremely powerful piece of gear that's located in Mission 7-6-6. You have to fight the

Magic Pot using the following attacks in this order: Gil Toss, Costly Punch, 99,999 Damage and Octaslash. The Genji Shield, when equipped, gives you permanent Omni Status Guard, absorbs elemental damage and keeps permanently active Barrier and MBarrier.

Genji Armor

Acquiring the Genji Armor requires you to complete your DMW gallery and to achieve 100% for each piece of the gallery. Genji Armor allows your max HP to reach 99,999, adding permanent Endure and Regen to Zack for as long as the gear is equipped.

Fast Materia Mastering

After leveling-up to a fairly high level (around the time you get the DMW called Lucky Stars), you're in a good position to master your equipped Materia rather easily. Head to the game's very first mission, which should be extremely easy for you to complete by this point. Because of the parameter breaks, dying there is unlikely. You can master your equipped Materia rather easily by hitting this mission up over and over again.

Following Aerith

There comes a time in the game where you need to follow Aerith around Midgar. If you're getting lost or are just feeling lazy, you can stand in front of her and she'll literally push you to where you need to go. Just be sure to steady yourself in front of her so that she doesn't walk past you.

Missiles in Banora

Early in the game, you'll reach a town called Banora. Near the end of the mission there, you'll encounter a weird little minigame where missiles will be shot towards you and you'll have to cut them down out of midair. This seems like a useless exercise, but in fact how many missiles you manage to halt will give you more time when you have to get back to Angeal's mom's house. What's more, you'll get items and other rewards for cutting the missiles down. If you use the added time to scour the town for more items and grab them all, you'll get an additional substantial reward, including an Ether, a Soma, an X-Potion, an Elixir and a Phoenix Down.

9,999 HP

If you want 9,999 HP, try the following. Fuse together two fully-leveled HP Up materias together, and fuse into the materia twenty-five Elixirs (you have to have the item-materia fusion skill to do this). The end result will be an HP Up+ materia with +360% HP (or around there). Elixirs are fairly rare items, but you can get the Elixirs you need by doing missions.

SP Conversion

If you're in need of SP, here's a good way to convert your materia to massive amounts of it. Take any status-raising materia (such as HP Up), and fuse it with a Chocobo Feather or another item that will raise the materia's attributes. Have the attribute added high (which shouldn't take too much SP), keeping in mind that the better-leveled the materia, the better this will work. Once you get the materia, convert it into SP.

By converting a materia like SP++ (30+) fully mastered, I got 150,000 SP. The rarer the materia converted, the more SP you will get from it.

Mission Difficulty

There are hundreds of optional missions in the game, and each and every one of them are worth your time. You'll get lots of special items, gear and materia for completing them, not to mention Gil and "experience" that will go towards leveling up. However, you may notice that there are difficulty levels affixed to each mission. Keep in mind that these fluctuate depending on your level, so if a mission is listed as "very hard" and you don't want to undertake it at the present time, it will become "hard" and then "normal" (and so on) as the difficulty level adjusts to your ever-raising level. This ultimately makes every mission in the game manageable at one point or another.

Find the Cursed Ring

At the very beginning of the game, after you fight Behemoth, you will be quickly brought to the second chapter. You'll have a scene with a character named Kunsel, who will brief you about all sorts of important stuff. He'll then tell you to check out the nearby supply pod, where you'll find a Bronze Bangle. However, if you check the pod again, and again, and again (twenty more times, in fact), you will find an item called the Cursed Ring.

The Cursed Ring is a statistical powerhouse, raising your HP, MP and SP by 10%, as well as increasing all stats by ten points. However, you can't use limit breaks, you can't level up, and you can't access the DWMs during battle, meaning it's both a blessing and a curse!

Avoiding Mission Battles

Most battles in missions can actually be avoided, if you know what to do. Simply hug walls while you're running through areas and battles should be easily avoided. This trick will always work in round-shaped rooms, though it has less of a chance of working in other situations.

New Game+

To unlock a New Game+ option, beat the game once through and save after the ending and credits have concluded. You can then play through the game again with your items, gear, Materia, and more from your previous quest.

WALKTHROUGH

Part 00: Prologue

Midgar

The game starts off innocuously enough with a series of cutscenes introducing the game's main character, Zack. Zack is a 2nd Class SOLDIER operative with great skill. You'll be introduced to his mentor, Angeal, as well. And yes, even Sephiroth can be seen in the game's opening minutes. When you finally gain control for the first time, you'll do battle with a number of weak enemies that will be nothing but fodder for your sword. Use this opportunity to adjust to the game's unique fighting system (this isn't Final Fantasy VII's turn-based fighting style), but rest assured it's next-to-impossible to die here. There is no failing.

After this battle concludes, you'll witness a few more cutscenes. When you regain control once more, Zack will run into a Behemoth.

Boss Battle - Behemoth

HP	MP	STEAL	DROP
7870	122	N/A	N/A

Unlike the last battle, this one is likely to challenge you a little bit (especially since you're almost certain to be unfamiliar with the game's control scheme), but we recommend dodging attacks as best you can while unleashing melee strikes coupled with Blizzaga.

All three offensive spells you have do a fair amount of damage, but ice-based spells work best on the fire-friendly Behemoth. Be especially wary of his tail attack, which is perhaps his most potent.

Part 01: Embrace Your Dreams

Shinra Building

Speaking with Kunsel again after you've read the e-mails will bring you to the corridor outside of the office. Follow him to the mission registration screen, where you can register to undertake the game's many optional missions. However, the first mission is far from optional. Approach the save point nearby after registering and save your game.

Then, hit Triangle to open your menu while standing on the save point and go to Missions. From there, select the "Shinra Electric Power Company" option, and then Training Missions, and then Shinra's Basic Training. This will be your very first mission undertaken in the game, and unlike the other numerous missions in the game, this one isn't optional. This mission is extremely easy (trust us -- they get a lot harder as the game progresses) and will pit you against eight Sentries. Just hack and slash your way through them for an easy victory, and remember that you can find more in-depth information on this guide's dedicated section for Missions.

You'll win an Elixir for your efforts. Speak to Kunsel again and he'll inform you that you can grab items out of the repositories nearby, and to check them often. Check them this time for a Bronze Bangle, which you should immediately equip for an HP boost. But, don't give up on searching here, because one of the game's biggest secrets will expose itself soon. If you search the same bin twenty more times (yes, twenty), Kunsel will tell you over and over again to stop being greedy. But finally, on the twentieth attempt, your buddy relents and hands over the Cursed Ring.

The Cursed Ring is a statistical dynamo, adding +10 to all of your statistics, and raising HP, MP and AP considerably. There's a catch, of course, and that is that you can't level up with it equipped. In other words, whenever it's equipped, you're cursed and your character's growth will be stagnated; only use the Cursed Ring under the right circumstances.

When you're prepared to leave, go back into the office and speak with Angeal to get going (Lazard will be heading out with you, too).

Wutai

You'll be automatically transported to Wutai, and before long, you'll find yourself under siege by a trio of Wutai Privates, who can easily be wiped out. When they are defeated, you can then begin heading down the linear pathway ahead of you. You'll have a few random encounters as you go, with Wutai Privates and Wutai Sergeants, but nothing you can't handle.

Mount Tamblin - Near Fort

When you get far enough up the pathway, you'll experience another seemingly-random cutscene with Angeal on the subject of a fruit called dumbapples. When you regain control thereafter, simply head down the next part of the linear path to a save point. You should save your game and be sure to read the e-mail Lazard sent out. Onto the next area.

Yet another cutscene ensues here as Zack and Angeal wait for their comrades in SOLDIER to set off a diversionary detonation that will allow Zack to infiltrate the compound. Once that explosion goes off, you'll be thrust into battle with a plethora of enemies. Thankfully, all of them are quite weak. It's difficult to count how many enemies tend to appear in battles like these since they consistently regenerate, but we counted about twenty Wutai Privates, a couple of Wutai Sergeants, and four well-placed Wutai Privates on the stone wall surrounding you.

Concentrate your attacks on the ground forces first and foremost. When they've been expelled, you can then use one of the two attack spells currently available to you to take out the privates firing from afar. When they are slain, you'll quickly be put into yet another battle on the other side of the door you just breached. After a quick (and easy) battle and an equally quick phone conversation with Angeal, you'll regain control. You'll see a series of eleven stars in the upper left corner of your screen. These stars will fill in as you kill enemies (which will impress Director Lazard).

Fort Tamblin - Corridor

Begin your romp through the fortress by heading left down the path (to the right is a dead end). You'll see a treasure chest, so grab the Soma out of it. Then, go right down the pathway, where another battle will likely ensue (this time with two Wutai Privates accompanied by a Foulander).

Continue along the linear pathway, killing any enemies that show themselves. When three Wutai gunners show themselves and fire down the corridor before fleeing, you know you're on the right path. Go down this path and enemies will come out of a trap door to your right to attack.

Once they're slain, examine the trap door they came through for even more enemies to fight. Then, after speaking with Lazard on the phone following the latter battle, continue along the linear path. If you run into a chest with a Potion in it shortly thereafter, you're on the right path. There's also a chest with an Ether in it back a ways and to your right, in a dead end alcove. You may be excited to see a nearby treasure chest to your left after acquiring the Potion, but that chest will actually cause three Wutai Privates and a Wutai Sergeant to appear on the scene.

After slaying them, head down the path, where you'll be assaulted by two Foulanders. Further up the path, a couple more Foulanders will attack accompanied by two lesser Wutai Privates. After eliminating that enemy party, be sure to grab the Hi-Potion from the treasure chest ahead, and then round the nearby corner. Two Wutai Privates and a Wutai Sergeant will order you to come fight them. Select "Charge!" from your options.

The Privates will retreat, leaving the Sergeant a sitting duck for your attacks. Once the Sergeant is defeated, continue down the pathway. As you approach a gate leading even further into the fortress, you will be assailed by three more Foulanders. Eliminate them, and then speak to Lazard on the phone once more. When given an option, choose to move further into the fortress, but before going through the door, be absolutely sure to backtrack just a little bit and grab the Ether from the chest.

Fort Tamblin - Courtyard

Once through the door, expect more battles with the upper echelon of enemies in the area (Foulanders and Wutai Sergeants). You can go either way, and should actually go both ways in order to find treasure chests containing a Hi-Potion and some Earrings (be sure to equip the Earrings for a mild boost to your magic power). Then approach the save point in the middle of the area. Read the e-mail you get en route, and then save and heal yourself. Proceed forward to the staircase nearby.

As you do, a familiar face from Final Fantasy VII appears. This is Yuffie in her younger days, and after a humorous scene with Zack, she'll run off. This will free you up to go forward and engage in a boss battle.

Boss Battle - Vajradhara Tai & Vajradhara Wu

HP	MP	STEAL	DROP
2900	22	Vit Up	N/A

HP	MP	STEAL	DROP
2900	22	HP Up	N/A

This boss battle is not with a single boss, but with two. They are identical looking creatures save for some coloring differences, but both attack relatively the same. However, they can use tandem attacks that make it absolutely vital to eliminate one. The attack they use, called Twin Tomahawk, is devastating enough that it necessitates the use of a Cure spell when hit with it. Kill one and Twin Tomahawk is no longer an issue.

When one is downed and you only have to concentrate on the other, you'll be able to bob and weave a little bit more to the point where you can get behind the remaining foe, not only to dodge his attacks (such as the Mace Boomerang), but also to hit him from behind, which inflicts massive damage when compared to hit points removed from frontal attacks.

Fort Tamblin - Animal Trail

When the foes are slain (remember -- healing is the real key in that battle), you'll be brought to another cutscene. A monster will appear, even more daunting and evil than the ones you just fought, but luckily for you another battle won't ensue. After you're "saved" (you'll see what we mean), you'll run into Lazard once more. After a conversation with he and Angeal, you'll be attacked by a party that is nameless (the enemies are each called "???"). They are stronger than any humanoid enemies you met earlier, but are still not that much of a challenge. Focus all of your offense on one at a time to down them efficiently and with ease.

Thereafter, another cutscene will occur, and more of these "???" soldiers will appear on-screen. But you won't have to deal with them (pretty similar, indeed, to how we didn't have to take care of the third monster just a little bit earlier). They will be taken care of for you. When you regain control, run forward to the save point. Be sure to heal your character and save your game. Then, run forward. You'll come across some corpses of bodies that you identify as not being of Wutai origins. And before you know it, you're thrust into another boss battle, against Ifrit this time.

Boss Battle - Ifrit

HP	MP	STEAL	DROP
6720	409	Atk Up	Assault Twister

Someone has summoned the powerful Ifrit, but it remains uncertain just who is the culprit. Regardless, you'll now have to deal with him, which is a nuisance in itself, but nothing you can't overcome. First thing's first -- Ifrit is solely fire-based, so using Blizzard against him is a fine idea, and one that should be considered with regularity (though you don't want to eat up your MP, since you'll need to cast Cure from time-to-time as well).

Otherwise, Ifrit is a powerful foe with fire-based and physical attacks which can quickly take you down if you're not quick to dodge and block. His Hellfire attack is especially potent, so be sure to be quick on the Cure spell (or on a Potion/Hi-Potion) when you begin to take a beating. Continue to keep the Blizzard spells falling on him and bob and weave his attacks, slashing away (preferably at his back or side for extra damage).

Ifrit seems all but defeated when he comes to attack again. As he does, though, Sephiroth steps in and saves the day. And just like that, after another cutscene, you're transported back to SOLDIER HQ.

Part 02: Betrayal?

Midgar

It's been about a month since the events in Wutai occurred. Angeal is AWOL and appears that he might be a traitor, while the revelation that Genesis is being cloned has concerned SOLDIER greatly. What's more, those SOLDIER operatives who went to Angeal's hometown to investigate rumors lost contact and could be dead. It's up to Zack, accompanied by Tseng (a Turk) to head to Angeal's hometown to see what's going on.

Before talking to Tseng to head out on the mission, make sure to hit the supply pods to find a free Thunder Materia (although if you've been doing missions, you probably have several by now). You can also head out to the Briefing Room, where you'll run into Kunsel. He'll bring you outside of the Shinra Building, where you can explore some of Midgar.

Sector 8 - Fountain

You should see a group of three ladies here. Speak to them for a short dialogue. After that, talk to Angeal fan to join the Keepers of Honor Fan Club. Then speak to the Genesis Fan to join the Red Leather Fan Club. You should be getting emails from both clubs from now on.

Loveless Avenue

Talk to the Shinra captain standing near the entrance. This will unlock Mission 1-2 in the missions menu. Next head north towards the center alley at the top of the area, and talk to the Genesis Fan to join the Loveless Study Group Club. That is all. Head back to base.

Shinra Building

You can look around the building if you like. Once done, go upstairs and use the elevator to get to the soldier floor. Make your way into the Materia room and chat with the scientists. This unlocks Mission 8-2 in the Missions menu. Go back to the briefing room and speak to Tseng.

Banora

After some cutscenes (discussing Sephiroth, as well as your next destination and things pertinent to your mission), you'll be thrust into battle as soon as you arrive at Banola. Do battle with the two G Assassins you're automatically thrust into battle with (they're pushovers, believe it or not, even though they are made from cloning the powerful Genesis). Then, continue up the main pathway (no need to backtrack). You'll get an e-mail from Kunsel as you go, and you'll have to do battle with some more G Assassins and Guard Hounds, but nothing too out of control.

After saving your game, head north a little bit more. A cutscene will ensue where Zack will automatically take care of some enemies before being baited into a boss battle with a robotic spider named Guard Spider. His regular attacks are somewhat innocuous (though they'll do damage to you if you're low level). His special attacks should be avoided, however. If he uses EM Field, get away from him, because it creates a damage field around him. Type 97 Cannon and Spider Web are projectile attacks that can be easily dodged. Flanking him for critical damage is preferable, but he moves fast, so it might not be possible. Thankfully, he's simply not that hard of a boss to defeat with conventional methods.

Grab the X-Potion from the nearby treasure chest. Save your game again if you like. Head for the exit near Tseng to proceed to the next area.

Banora Village

After the battle concludes and the brief cutscene finishes thereafter, heal Zack if he needs it, and then run towards the wreckage of the Guard Spider. When you do, Tseng will talk to you briefly and then you will gain control yet again. Push forward, speak to Tseng one more time, and then run into the adjacent area. Tseng and Zack will find themselves in a deep cutscene yet again, so pay attention!

After this last cutscene, you're free to explore the area. Tseng will give you directions to find Angeal's house, but before you do that, be sure to explore the area to the left of Tseng and the grave he's examining. You'll find a Hi-Potion in a treasure chest there. Once acquired, you can then head down the path towards the group of houses ahead. Run to the houses and begin tackling them from left to right.

The first house on the left side of the semi-circle can be accessed, but be sure to grab the Remedy from the treasure chest to the right of the entrance before attempting to go in. When you do, a Blood Taste will run out and attack you. Kill him and move on to the next house on the other side of the well (since the door will be locked after killing the foe).

This is a house you can enter. Coincidentally, it's also Angeal's house, and when you enter, a cutscene with Angeal's mother will take place. Watch it, and you'll regain control of Zack after it has run its course. Before leaving the house, be sure to explore it (you can examine the Buster Sword, some pictures, and a treasure chest with 5 Gil.

After doing all of that, head back outside. You'll do battle with a trio of G Assassins automatically when you walk outside (the gate that was keeping you from accessing the next area has been removed). After killing them, backtrack to Angeal's house and use the save point next to his house (it's better to be safe than sorry). Then, go through the area where the gate used to be. You'll have more battles here leading up to a fork in the road. Take the right part of the fork, grabbing the Hi-Potion and MP Up Materia as you go forward to a cliff where Tseng is waiting for you.

Banora Factory

Speak with Tseng to learn more about the mission and why Sephiroth chose you to undertake it (and why he, in turn, refused). You'll then automatically find yourself infiltrating the source of the Genesis clones. You'll be thrust into yet another battle with G Assassins, so take the foes out. Then, after a cutscene with Tseng, check your e-mail (it's from Director Lazard). Though you'll first want to go towards the stairs where Tseng is, be absolutely sure you go in the other direction first. At the end of the metal catwalk is a treasure chest containing 500 Gil.

After grabbing the loot, head back to where you were originally and go down the stairs towards the location Tseng was at during the latest cutscene. Continue down the next flight of stairs and another battle will take place. This time, seven G Assassins and a Heli Gunner will make themselves seen. Keep in mind that G Assassins will constantly spawn until all seven appear and are killed -- therefore, take out the Heli Gunner first. That foe is the bigger threat of the two types of enemies, anyway.

When the enemy threat is nullified, run forward and to the left (so that you're underneath the series of catwalks we previously traversed). You'll find a treasure chest containing an Elixir there. After grabbing it, you can then head to your right, where a door leading into the next area can be found. In this small room, grab the Remedy from the chest on your right, and then go forward into the next room. Yet another cutscene will ensue at this point. It's brief, however, so you'll be able to use the save point in the room before continuing on. Again, better safe than sorry.

Here, another epic cutscene will take place with Genesis, Angeal and Tseng. As the story continues to unravel before you very eyes, you'll see Genesis attack Tseng, Zack go after Genesis, and Angeal stop him from doing so as Genesis and Angeal both leave the building. You'll then regain control back in the room where Tseng was examining the computer. You'll pass by the same save point you used earlier, so feel free to use it again. Then, head back into the large warehouse room.

At this point, Tseng will show back up, killing enemies and telling you to leave immediately. Take his advice and do just that. Once back outside, however, look to your right to find a different-looking treasure chest containing a Bronze Armlet. An X-Potion can also be found on the far side of the warehouse in a similar looking treasure chest, so be sure to grab that as well before dashing down the path back towards the village.

Banora Village

When you approach the gate to the village, a weird scene will occur where you have to cut down enemy shells being launched at the village. You need to press X when the shell begins to light up and the fuse ignites in order to cut the shell in half, nullifying its effect as shown in the tutorial All ten can hit Zack, and he won't be damaged. How many you destroy affects what comes next. Consider this an exercise in hand-eye coordination. You get 1000 Gil from it, plus 500 Gil if you manage to chain a 10-hit combo.

After this exercise, Tseng will hit up Zack on his cell phone telling him the airstrike is imminent. Remember all the glowing spots on the ground, where Zack says he'll check them out later? You have between twenty-five seconds to one minute (depending on how many shells you've destroyed) to dash back into town and touch all these spots. Depending on how many spots you've touched and how many shells you destroyed, you will get items like potions, and Gil. When the timer is up, it takes you right to Angeal's mom's house. When you arrive at the door, Tseng will again call Zack telling him that he's delayed the airstrike temporarily, but to hurry. And with that, Zack enters the house to find Angeal's mother dead. Angeal and Genesis then make their getaway. Just what's going on here? Well, that remains to be seen. What doesn't remain to be seen, however, is Genesis' summon -- Bahamut.

Boss Battle - Bahamut

HP	MP	STEAL	DROP
8720	424	Hi-Potion	Force Bracelet

The battle with Bahamut will vary greatly depending on how powerful Zack is at the present time (though this is a statement that could be used throughout the game). Unlike many battles you've fought thusfar, Bahamut will move around a great deal, jumping up and down off and on screen. These jumps do damage to you simply by shaking the ground, so try to stay far away from him when these events occur to minimize damage taken. Also try to stay away from the front of his body, since he often swings his claws. His one major special attack is Mega Flare, a Final Fantasy staple, and is an attack that can't be avoided, so be sure to have your Cure Materia ready. Otherwise, flank him for critical damage and keep healed to avoid any sudden catastrophies.

Part 03: Monster

Midgar

This section of the game begins with Zack back at Shinra HQ in Midgar. After having some time with himself thinking about Angeal and his current whereabouts, he gets a call on his cell phone. It's Sephiroth, and he wants to see Zack in Director Lazard's office. When you regain control, you'll also get an e-mail from Kunsel, so make sure to read it on the way.

Optionally, as you head towards the office, you will come across the Training Room (you may have explored this place earlier). The guard outside of the door will let you know that there's an experiment going on inside, and while he can't stop you from going in, he asks you not too. Naturally, you should ignore him and head inside, where the mad scientist Hojo can be found. By speaking with him and agreeing to help him with his experiment, you'll be pitted against three different weak enemy "programs" before being put in a fourth battle against Experiment #88, a Hojo creation. This creature actually packs a powerful punch (and can attack with his tail, making it annoying to critically attack him from behind), but can be easily felled. Do so -- you'll understand why later.

Feel free to walk around the rest of the area (or head down to Midgar, if you so desire). Ultimately, though, the Briefing Room is your target. Grab the Star Pendant from the repositories in the first room (remember -- you can't get any more items here until the next chapter commences) and then go into the next room, where a 2nd and 3rd Class will be arguing with one another. Be sure to speak with the 3rd after the 2nd leaves in a huff. With that event in the bag, you'll unlock Mission 7-1 in the Missions menu.

Sector 8 - Fountain

Make your way to the upper level, and talk to the guy by the wall at the top of the stairs. This will unlock Mission 2-1 in the Missions menu.

Shinra Building

After that, head back out and to the elevators. You can take these elevators up to Director Lazard's office (Kunsel will come out and talk to you as you approach the elevators). Once up to Lazard's office, it won't take long for him to cut to the chase -- you're being promoted to 1st Class! Though Zack is lacking excitement about it right now, you'll be asked to change into a 1st's uniform (which will happen automatically). There's better news, though. Not only will you get two more Materia slots, but you'll also be able to fuse materia for the first time (and you'll be given Fire Materia and Blizzard Materia in order to attempt your first fusion). By the way, by fusing those two materia, you'll get Thunder Materia.

You can pick the scientist's brain about fusion more, or you can decline. Either way, he'll leave you, at which point you'll get a call from Lazard. He'll summon you back to his office. You'll also get three new tutorial e-mails about Materia Fusion and a disturbing e-mail listing both Angeal and Genesis as "killed in action". Regardless, head back to the elevator and back to Director Lazard's office. After a brief discussion of your upcoming mission, which will include the assistance of Sephiroth, alarms begin to rage all around you. There's an invasion alert. Lazard orders Sephiroth to protect the president while Zack is ordered to the entrance.

Quickly use the nearby save point to save your game, and then proceed to the door, where you'll be asked if you want to proceed. The elevator will be stopped on the forty-ninth floor, however. If you choose to proceed to the entrance, though, you will be brought there in short order.

It's chaos on the first floor, with machines and Genesis copies attacking with regularity. It seems a rogue Shinra scientist named Hollander might be responsible for the attack. A Sweeper and a G Avenger will approach and attack, but they can be taken out easily. It's the subsequent battle that poses a greater threat, because you will be attacked by eighteen enemies (though not all at once). Six will be Sweepers, six will be Avengers, and six will be weak robotic enemies called Red Saucers. You can make quick work of them if you're high enough in level, though you will want to make sure you concentrate on the Sweepers first and foremost, as they are the most powerful enemies. The Red Saucers will not appear until the end of the battle, however, and the battle will be capped off by four of the six Sweepers showing up simultaneously.

Loveless Avenue

Once those foes are all eliminated, another cutscene will ensue. You'll meet up with some new Turks, who are calling Sector 8 security for themselves. As you attempt to help them out, you'll be introduced to a new character named Cissnei. She'll run off, as will Tseng and the rest of the Turks present, leaving you to your own devices. What should you do? Well, for starters, run forward to LOVELESS Avenue... but be aware that you'll begin running into random encounters at this point. (And as a reminder, remember to equip two more materia into your new slots).

Once on LOVELESS Avenue, look to your right and to your left. Enemies are attacking civilians on both sides. Head to the right and help the woman and her child fend off a Red Saucer and a Sweeper. They'll give you an Amulet for your help. On the left, a man will need help taking out a Sweeper and his G Avenger companion. For your assistance, he'll hand over some Earrings. Then, run down the avenue, where a cutscene will take place. Cissnei is under attack from a rather powerful, shotgun and nightstick-toting Genesis copy. It's time to step in and help her out.

This foe, even if you're under-leveled (and we are far from such) should be a pushover. He's armed with a shotgun in one hand and a nightstick in the other, but it's his shotgun that he's going to favor much more. Whenever he chooses to shoot his firearm, he'll shoot it twice, and the damage can amount to something substantial. His special attack, Scorcher, is an unavoidable version of his classic shotgun attack (though his regular attacks are hard to dodge on their own). You're actually better off blocking his attack in an attempt to nullify the damage dealt as opposed to dodging them outright. Either way, flanking him is going to be hard, so you'll have to deal with hitting him with normal attacks. Keep the damage slow but steady (Fira seems to work well on him).

When the battle is over, the Genesis copy will attempt an escape, but Zack will have none of it. Was that the real Genesis? Likely not, but we still can't be too sure. As Zack examines the corpse, Cissnei returns and a conversation ensues. For helping her out, she'll hand over the Research Dept. QMC, which will give you access to a new shop (this shop sells materia you don't have yet, like the ultra-useful Esuna, so be sure to grab it when you can). Then, Sephiroth asks Zack to head to the Mako Reactor.

Mako Reactor 5

You'll arrive at the reactor automatically, and once there, you should save your game before proceeding. As soon as you begin to walk away from the save point, another boss battle will be presented to you.

This is a simple boss fight. The most difficult part of the boss fight isn't actually the battle but rather the lack of area to maneuver around. Because you're fighting on a catwalk, maneuvering around won't really be possible to the extent that you'd like. Regardless, this creature is a pushover. Slash away at him, attempting to get behind him to deal critical damage if possible. The only attack of his you'll want to be weary of is his Dragoon-like Jump attack, which can be dodged with proper timing.

When A-Sahagin is downed, a series of lengthy cutscenes will ensue. You'll see just how close Sephiroth, Angeal and Genesis were to each other, to the point that they would epically duel in the battle simulator… while reading poetry! After watching the long cutscene, you'll be transported back to the reactor, where Sephiroth and Zack will come to the conclusion that Genesis and Angeal are indeed in league with the rogue scientist Hollander. And just like that, you're given control once more.

Backtrack slightly to the save point, where you should save your game once more. Then, head forward and follow along this linear pathway until you reach Sephiroth (you may notice that you'll be fighting A-Sahagins here, which were just the previous boss battle -- so be careful!) To Sephiroth's left is a ladder, but if you attempt to go down, you'll see that the ladder isn't fully extended, making it impossible. Instead, continue right from Sephiroth's location then down another linear pathway.

You'll come across a wheel that, when activated, will lower a path to your right, leading to another series of catwalks. This effectively connects the previous area for possible ease later. Then, head to the left of the switch, where a ladder will lead you downward. Head along the path forward -- you'll see Sephiroth waiting by a door ahead. When you speak with him, he'll let you know that the door ahead needs to be powered by Mako, necessitating a long climb downward to the reactor's ground floor. At this point, backtrack to the previous ladder and climb back up.

That path we just lowered earlier can now be used. Once across, head left to the save point. Save your game before heading along the other branch of the newly-accessible catwalk. When you reach the wall, you can either head right or left. Opt to head left to the ladder, and climb down to the area below. Head forward to the next ladder, but head left down the path before reaching the ladder to reach yet another ladder leading down.

Head forward to the Mako control unit ahead. Before examining it, search to the left and to the right of it, where treasure chests can be found. To the left, you'll find a Hi-Potion, while to the right, you'll find an accessory called Shinra Alpha. The latter item is something you'll almost certainly want to equip. After grabbing both items, you can then examine the Mako control unit to restore power to the door above. With that done, you can then backtrack all the way back to that door, to meet with Sephiroth.

Plate Interior - Secret Factory

The Mako control unit has granted us access to a super-secret lab. Speak with Sephiroth once inside and he'll tell you of secret documents that must be examined. Coincidentally, the camera will also pan behind each of the three documents you need to examine to make your life easier. Next to Sephiroth is the summary of an experiment called Project G. On the other side of the room, near a save point, you'll find a report on something called the SOLDIER Degradation Phenomenon. And finally, near the staircase you'll read an outline for something called The Ancients Project. Keep in mind that each document triggers a dialogue and cutscene.

After examining all three documents, speak with Sephiroth again. After speaking briefly, Hollander will show up in his lab, finding Sephiroth and Zack there. Shortly thereafter, Genesis shows up, one wing and all. Genesis refuses Sephiroth to go after Hollander, but as Hollander runs off, Sephiroth orders Zack to pursue him. You'll now go after Hollander.

Plate Interior

Head forward along the pathway when you regain control, and go left through an open door that wasn't open previously. As you head through into the next area, you'll see Hollander running off in the distance (this will let you know that you're on the right track). There's no imminence in pursuing him, though, which is a good thing since you'll be running into enemy parties en route. Do save your game before you proceed.

The great thing about this part which makes it easier is that if you go in the wrong direction, the game will tell you and you'll be redirected. So as you head forward down the path, swing left through the open door, but don't worry if you miss it, because the game will let you know. Once you run into this room, though, you'll see Hollander hiding behind a door, and he'll run off to the previous area. Chase after him. It'll seem like he's almost in reach, but then an enemy party intercepts you, allowing him to increase his lead. After eliminating them, proceed down the pathway to a staircase. You'll come across a classic fork in the road at this point.

First, head to your right. This isn't where Hollander went, but at the end of this pathway, you'll find a treasure chest. Crack it open to find two Hi-Potions to add to your inventory. Then, go in the other direction. Eventually, you'll see Hollander ahead once again, but resist the urge to chase him just for a moment as you look to your right, where another treasure chest can be found. Crack it open to find MAG Up Materia. Proceed on thereafter to chase after him. It's all linear and impossible to get lost, but you will be facing off with enemy parties regardless.

When you reach the next area of the reactor, Zack will call out to Hollander, but he'll just run away, forward and to the right. Before chasing him, run forward and to the left. Ascend some stairs and you'll secure a Circlet from the treasure chest. After grabbing it, backtrack and go in the direction Hollander fled. As you proceed down a long set of stairs, use the save point ahead. Pursue Hollander again to a boss encounter.

These three robots, created by Hollander, are a bit of a nuisance since they're so attack-heavy. However, it should be nothing you can't handle at this point in the game. Differentiating between the three robots is really a fruitless endeavor, because none really takes presidence over the other. Cutter Machine is a melee-heavy machine, while Shot Machine uses machineguns and missiles. Pile Machine is a mixture of the two. Try to bunch them together to hit multiple targets simultaneously, and since you'll likely be poisoned during the course of the battle, have some Remedies handy to take care of that mid-fight. Otherwise, the fight gets much easier once one machine, and then two are downed. Button mash to survive.

After the fight, Angeal will appear, and he too has one wing, just like Genesis. In the course of the brief conversation between Angeal and Zack, Zack appeals to him not to look at himself as a monster, but as an angel. Angeal won't have any of it, however, and attacks Zack. When Zack won't defend himself, he attacks again. Chapter 3 complete.

Part 04: An Angel's Dream

Midgar

Zack's epic fall from the previous chapter concludes here, when he lands in a destroyed church. The nearby girl is Aerith (Aeris from Final Fantasy VII), and she is quite protective of her flowerbed naturally growing there. The reason for this is simple -- flowers are a rare commodity in an industrialized city such as Midgar, and Zack concurs, telling Aerith that she can make a load of money selling them to the citizenry. When you gain control, open the chest in the back left corner for a couple of Ethers.

After grabbing these items, go towards the entrance/exit of the large church. Aerith will intercept you, however, and ask to go with you. She'll lead you out of the slums. Zack agrees, and you'll find yourself back outside. As you head forward following her, you'll get an e-mail announcing your recent promotion to 1st Class. Nice! Continue to follow Aerith. When she stops, speak to her. She'll tell you she wants to plant some flowers and keep moving. This will take you to the next area.

Sector 5 Slums - Market

When you regain control after the short dialogue, head for the southern exit. Talk to the people here for information as to where the pickpocket kid went. Everyone here will be conspiring against you, so don't expect them to be of any help. But be sure to go ahead and ask around anyway.

Start out by speaking to the gift shop clerk, then to the little girl at the bottom of the area. Next, talk to the kid by the market entrance, then to the guy running the "materia" shop. Lastly, have a chat with the "Shopping Paradise" clerk. Now go speak to Aerith who is waiting near the materia shop. Head to where the Shinra infantryman is, for a story event.

Now that you have your wallet back, you get to choose how you want to help the boy. I chose the to get his wallet back from the monster. Anyway, head for the streets outside the market and head north. Beat the worms. At the market, talk to the Shopping Paradise clerk to whip up a perfume for Aerith. "Drip" = 1 drop and "Splash" = 10 drops. Press X to shut off the tap once the number of drops match what the clerked had asked.

Now head to the gift shop and the guy will give you a Soma, a Remedy and a Hi-Potion. The conversation is cut short when Lazard calls Zack and tells him to make his way back to the Shinra Building, as Genesis has launched another attack. Getting back to the building can be a little bit of a pain, however, so follow these directions. Go forward back to the previous area, and then back to the area where your wallet was stolen. Go to the far end of this area, where a gate leading back to the surface can be found (you weren't allowed to use it earlier). The boy who stole your wallet finds you just before you can leave. His gift? The Steal Materia.

Sector 0 - Highway

When on the other side of the gate, the Shinra Building can be seen in the distance, but getting there is another story entirely. As you run forward, save your game, and then proceed onward. It won't be long until you're assailed by the first enemy party, called G Assailants. There are three of them, but they are pushovers (just dodge their knife throwing ability if used). The second enemy party to appear are two Moth Slashers. These enemies are peskier than the G Assailants, but they're still pushovers. Their Drill Attack can be mildly devastating, so be sure to dodge it.

The third enemy party to attack are more G Assailants, but this time there isn't three of them, there's six. There could be twenty, theoretically, and one fact wouldn't change -- they're still pushovers. This party of six should be and will be quickly dispatched. The next enemy that appears is a boss.

The G Warrior stands alone in battle, but he still isn't all that powerful. The one ability that he uses more than any other in battle happens to be one of the peskier afflictions in the game, however, and that is Silence. If he manages to land his spell on you, you won't be able to cast magic, and this can be a problem. If you have a Remedy handy and you are silenced, make sure to use it to remove its plague. Otherwise, the G Warrior has standard melee attacks that are easily dodged, and his HP is not insurmountable. An overall easy battle, but a notable one nonetheless.

When the battle concludes, Zack and Angeal meet. Zack appeals to Angeal, and Angeal appeals right back. Zack, oddly enough, chooses to help Angeal even though he has no idea what he's up to. And just like that, Angeal grabs Zack and flies towards Shinra HQ. Once there, they meet up with Sephiroth, and assignments are dished out. While Sephiroth and Angeal go handle business elsewhere, it's up to Zack to head up to the science laboratory to take care of, that is protect Professor Hojo.

Shinra Building

When you regain control, save your game via the save point on your left. Then, head forward along the corridor. It may be extremely tempting to take the first path you come across heading rightward, but resist the urge. While you can go through the door at the end of the corridor, each and every door beyond it is locked up. It is simply a complete waste of your time. Instead, proceed forward and go into the adjoining area.

There's not a lot to see here, so swing right into the room. Grab the chest on the left side of the elevator to acquire an X-Potion, and hit up the chest on the right side for a Remedy. Then, approach the elevator. When it lets you out, you'll be in the same room as Hojo. Save your game at the save point and then speak with Hojo. To catalyze the next cutscene, however, you'll need to talk to him again and accept his challenge.

At this point, Angeal and Genesis both show up, and a rather interesting cutscene takes place. Hojo seems untouched by what's going on around him, and the battle between Angeal and Genesis continues. As Genesis makes his escape, Angeal grabs Zack and chases after him. But to keep Angeal busy, Genesis summons a powerful monster. Zack is dropped in to fight the summoned creature as Angeal takes care of business.

Boss Battle - Bahamut Fury

HP	MP	STEAL	DROP
18000	312	Hi-Potion	Thundara

This creature is large. So large, in fact, that he doesn't move during battle. Rather, he rests at the side of a platform, waiting for you to come up to him to attack him. Magic is essentially nullified when used on him so you'll be forced to use physical attacks. Getting close to him is dangerous, though, because his regular swiping attacks won't only knock you back, but they'll damage you for a good amount as well. He has two primary attacks -- Hexafang and Exaflare -- both are devastating and unavoidable,.

Exaflare is especially powerful, with the ability to do 4,000 HP of damage easily. Because of these powerful attacks, go for broke to eliminate him as quickly as humanly possible. Even though he is huge and scary looking, he's not stacked with HP, so a well-planned battle only takes a short time.

Part 05: Where Are You?

Midgar

Before heading to Modeoheim, there's a lot of optional quests and excursions you can undertake. To trigger the Modeoheim sequence as part of the main story, you have to try to go visit Aerith at the bombed-out church. So simply head there (you'll meet Angeal en route) and speak with Tseng when you arrive if you want to skip ahead. Otherwise, read below and try to undertake a few of (or better yet all) these side quests.

At the Shinra Building, enter the briefing room and check the supply pods to get a Fira Materia. There are some new missions available for you to clear as well. Head for the Training Room next and speak to one of the scientists there to play the squats mini-game. Just press X at the right time to perform squats continuously. You must have performed more squats than your opponent after one minute to win. The rewards for winning are:

- Shinra Infantryman: Shinra Lunch Cart Specs

- Shinra Captain: Shinra Ceramic

- SOLDIER 3rd Class: Shinra Treads

- SOLDIER 2nd Class: Shinra Solder

After that, enter the Briefing Room once you clear missions 7-1-1 to 7-1-6. You will then be rewarded with the Premium Tires when the dialogue ends. Next, go to the Materia Room and hand over the mako stones that you have collected from the Mako Stones missions (8-2). The researchers there can generate some good Materia from them. Finally, take the elevator down to the entrance and speak to the City Planner Director. This will unlock Mission 6-2 in the Missions menu. Exit to Sector 8 afterwards.

Sector 8 - Fountain

Complete mission 2-1-1 first and head for the upper level of the area, then speak to the man standing near the stairs. Proceed to Loveless Avenue and speak to the Shinra army captain near the entrance. Complete missions 1-2-1 to 1-2-6 and he will give you the Craftsman Monthly. Speak to the Genesis Fan at the north alley as well. Return to Sector 8 and talk to the SOLDIER 2nd class and help him catch the Wutai spies. You must speak to each person three times to blow their cover.

- 1st Spy: The man at the northwest portion of Loveless Avenue.

- 2nd Spy: The Shinra infantryman at the Sector 5 Slums Market.

- 3rd Spy: The man coming out of the elevator at Shinra HQ 1F.

- 4th Spy: The woman at the upper level of Sector 8 Fountain.

- 5th Spy:e man in front of the rocket in Shinra Building Exhibit Room.

- 6th Spy: The boy in the Sector 6 Slums Park.

This unlocks Missions 4-3-1 to 4-3-6. You will also get the Walnut Wood. Now talk to the lady in the Slums Park. She is a member of the Silver Elite Sephiroth fan club. Select the following responses:

Question 1: Masamune. Question 2: Super Nova. Question 3: Left Hand. This makes you a member of the Silver Elite Fan Club.

Sector 5 Slums - Market

Speak to the little girl at the southeast corner of the area to unlock Mission 2-1-3. Next, talk to the guy running Item World to play yet another mini-game. All you have to do is pick up all 20 pieces of materia scattered around the market in the shortest possible time.

Exit out to the streets and take the west exit towards the Church Entrance for some cut-scenes. Then you'll regain control in a new area.

Modeoheim

Proceed forward to the save point ahead of you, where you can save your game, do any necessary shopping, and even access some missions if you so desire. Then, head down the linear pathway. There are no items to find, and no way to get lost, but you may run into an enemy encounter or two, so be prepared for that. When you reach the next area of the ravine you're traversing, a cutscene will occur where Zack will hit it off with one of the soldiers accompanying him on his journey. As Zack asks the guy's name, he takes off his helmet. Who did you think it was!? It's Cloud!

When you regain control, simply head through yet another patch of snowy terrain. Again, it's linear, and again, there are no items to find. When you reach some broken, tattered pipeline coming out of the snow and rockface, you'll know you're on the right track. Head into the next area.

Another cutscene will ensue here. Below is an abandoned mako factory that's been taken over by Genesis and his clone forces. As the small party reflects on what to do next, Tseng orders Zack to go and check things out. When you regain control, head rightward down the sloping pathway, and use the save point you encounter (better safe than sorry!) When you approach the outer entrance to the facility, you'll be asked what to do next. Select the topmost option, which will bring up a screen telling you how to stealthily infiltrate the factory. Read these instructions carefully!

Basically, you have a body temperature that's displayed in Celsius (how un-American!). You start at 36.5 degrees, and can't reach 26.0 degrees, or you'll be unable to move. Pressing X in sequence will allow you to do squats (kind of like you did in the exercise back at Shinra HQ) which will raise your temperature. Pressing the Circle button will allow you to crouch down behind various things to hide you from enemy sight.

This isn't as hard as it seems (believe us). You shouldn't even have to worry about doing your squats to raise your internal temperature. Instead, concentrate on heading rightward around the exterior of the factory. This is easily done, simply because there's only three guards outside, and they all come together right in front of the entrance. When they do, book inside and run rightward. They might see you, but keep running to avoid a battle (and subsequently having to do this over again). By going right around the outside of the factory, you'll find a huge door leading inside.

Mako Excavation Facility

You're now inside the factory. At the bottom of the stairs to the west is an X-Potion. Head right to the stairs which will lead you to the next area. You will have random encounters here, just like outside, but they're basically the same enemies -- G Battlers and G Attackers. The Attackers are fodder for your sword, but the Battlers are forces to be reckoned with.

They move fast, but commit themselves to attacks, so once they do, quickly dodge and flank them for critical damage.Continue down the staircase. Yet another save point can be seen on your right (this is a pretty friendly game as far as save points are concerned, eh?) After saving your game, proceed leftward, and swing around to the elevator. Examine it to take it to the next necessary area. At this point, a cutscene ensues. Hollander is nearly killed by Genesis, but Zack arrives on-scene in the nick of time. As Hollander tries to escape, Cloud temporarily stops him while Genesis and Zack speak. After Hollander runs off, Cloud pursues him, and Genesis and Zack do battle in a cutscene.

Boss Battle - Genesis

HP	MP	STEAL	DROP
14800	525	Elixir (x2)	MBarrier

Genesis can be a pesky foe to defeat depending on your level. We were in the low-30s when we fought him, so he was a pushover, but if you haven't done a lot of missions up to this point, this battle can be more difficult for you. Genesis isn't packing a lot of HP, but he does have some lethal attacks. His Dark Energy attack is a high-powered fire attack, while his Black Flurry attack is an unavoidable status-inflicting fray. If he uses the latter, make sure to use a Remedy straight away, as being cursed by that attack will guarantee that your DMW doesn't function. Other than some healing and gray magic (such as Magic Defense, which will alert you to the fact that using offensive magic here might not be a good idea), Genesis will concentrate on sword combos. These are easily dodged or blocked, but the former is preferable, since it will allow you to sustain no damage while repositioning yourself in relation to Genesis's position.

hen the battle is over, Genesis makes his dramatic getaway. Tseng, Cloud and Zack then find themselves back outside the factory we just infiltrated. If you explored the area surrounding the factory earlier, you would have noticed a cave entrance blocked by substantial ice buildup. The ice has been largely cleared away by this point, however, and you can now go through this cave, closer and closer to our target, Modeoheim.

On the other side of the cave (which happens instantaneously), you'll see a save point ahead and to your left (again, too many save points!) Save your game yet again, and then read the e-mail you receive. You'll learn that Modeoheim has been largely abandoned along with the Shinra attempts to mine mako in the area. The e-mail speculates that because of the abandoned status of the area, you may just find that anti-Shinra "elements" will call this place home. Remember this and head to town.

The path in the town will swing right down a gently-sloping hill. Be sure to grab the MP Up Materia from the treasure chest sitting on an abandoned house's porch before swinging right. As you head towards the temple-like structure ahead, Lazard will e-mail you. Be sure to read it as you head forward, and collect the Blizzara Materia from the treasure chest before proceeding into the temple-like structure, that is the Bathhouse

Modeoheim - Bathhouse

What will no doubt immediately grab your attention as you head into this dimly-lit, dank structure are the two bright white treasure chests ahead of you. Go forward and grab both -- out of the left, you should pick up an Ether, while from the right you should score a Hi-Potion. After both items are added to your inventory, head back to the entrance and take the only way out of this initial room via the pathway on your left.

After fighting Genesis, the A-Griffon is likely to give you the giggles, but nonetheless it's still a boss battle you'll have to contend with. He can mix up his spells and will cast them almost exclusively (he can cast attack spells like Fira and gray magic like Silence), but when he wants to attack physically, be sure to dodge his talons. There's really not much else to say here. If you defeated Genesis, which you obviously did if you're here, than the A-Griffon should be nothing more than a glamorized pushover.

When you regain control following the brief boss battle, turn to your left and grab the Ether from the treasure chest alongside the staircase leading up. Then run up the stairs and watch the ensuing cutscene. Cloud is lying on the floor unconscious, but Zack wakes him up and runs into an injured Tseng thereafter. Head through the door next to Tseng when you regain control, and go down the stairs you encounter. Head right around the stairs after descending them, and head to the next staircase leading up Grab the Force Bracelet from the chest under the stairs.

Once up the stairs, ignore the machinery in front of you and go through the gaping hole on the right side. This will bring you outside. Run forward along the gigantic pipes in front of you, and bear rightward through another hole and back into the building. Follow the brief linear pathway once back inside, which will ultimately lead to a cutscene. Here, Hollander, Angeal and Zack will have an extended conversation that uncovers more of the storyline. And before you know it, you're thrust into a boss battle with, of all people, Angeal himself. A very monstrous, ill-formed Angeal.

Boss Battle - Angeal Penance

HP	MP	STEAL	DROP
27800	544	Bronze Armlet	Lightning Armlet

You'll notice when you fight Angeal Penance a rather interesting motif to his attacks. They're all modeled after the Seven Deadly Sins, and most of them have a special attack tied to the sin (with the exception of Gluttony, which is actually a healing spell, Defense of Lust, which is a defensive booster, and Envy, which is gray magic). The four actual attacks are as follows. Wings of Pride is a projectile attack that's hard to dodge, so you're better off blocking it. Rage of Sloth is a one-hit, weak lightning spell that is easy to dodge (but getting hit by it shouldn't shatter your game). Charge of Greed is an attack that can be dodged, but that is quite lethal if it hits.

And Unleashed Wrath, the deadliest of them all, is an unavoidable attack that can completely destroy you in one hit. As a result, keep yourself healed at all times. If you're not healed, you're going to die. We were extremely well-leveled here (in the low 30s) and still found ourselves being heavily damaged by many of this foe's attacks, leaving us wondering how badly he will decimate any player who hasn't undertaken the numerous missions we already have. Be on the defensive here, and try to balance your attacks with a plenty of healing and evasion. Angeal Penance is stronger than Genesis, there's simply no doubt about that.

Part 06: Protect Your Honor

Junon

This mission begins innocuously enough, but it won't remain so for long. Soaking in the sun on the beach during a prolonged vacation from his SOLDIER-related duties, Zack is soon joined by Cissnei, the female member of the Turks we met earlier. They'll discuss some things, and then Tseng shows up on the scene. At this time, G Divers will come out of the water. However, armed with only a beach umbrella and your bathing suit, it seems like the odds are stacked against you.

Strangely, however, nothing really changes. You're as strong as you are with a sword equipped, and your defense doesn't suffer at all, even though Zack is without a shirt. Go figure. The G Divers will appear both out of the water and around the beach near the water, so watch your back. They have Fin Kicks and some gun attacks, but they're pushovers. It's their numbers that are more daunting than anything else here.

Lower Junon

When the fight is over (which will happen when you've slain the prerequisite number of G Divers) you'll rapidly be transported to another town that Final Fantasy VII fans should be plenty familiar with -- Junon. Upon arrival, you'll immediately be assailed by two G Troopers, who shouldn't give you too hard of a time. Following that battle, a cutscene will ensue, and then you'll finally gain full control over your character.

Quickly run forward to the save point on your right and save the game. Then, run forward. Random battles will ensue here, but they'll all happen with G Troopers, so you shouldn't have many issues. You'll also encounter an extended battle similar to the one that just took place on the beach, with the enemy refreshing itself several times over. Be prepared for that battle, since it can challenge you unlike a normal random conflict would.

As you head up this street, you'll also want to make sure to grab some treasure. The first chest you'll encounter will be on your right, and it contains a staggering 5,000 Gil. Further up the street on the left, a Hi-Potion can be acquired. And finally, at the end of the street, to the left of the elevator you have to take up to continue, you can acquire a Bronze Armlet. After those items are acquired, take the elevator up.

You'll encounter a Genesis copy up here that is stronger than most others you've encountered so far, but because you'll fight many of them up here, it's not a boss battle. These enemies are called G Bladers, and they're equipped with Squall-like gun swords (ala Final Fantasy VIII). However, these gun swords are revolvers that pack a powerful punch. Their primary attack is called Gunblade (how clever), though they are also capable of casting some moderately powerful magic, such as Fira.

Thankfully, these guys aren't too quick, especially when they commit to the Gunblade attack, so flanking them to deal critical damage is rather easy, making any fight with them exceptionally manageable.

When the initial threat is subdued, you can continue along the street. Chances are, you won't run into any random encounters here, but there are pre-set battles with more G Bladers and some of their lesser G Trooper friends, so be prepared for more fighting. You'll also see Hollander running away during a brief cutscene, so you know that you'll be pursuing him yet again, just like you did earlier in Midgar. In addition to Hollander dashing off and the pre-set battles, you'll also want to keep an eye out for two treasures. On your right, you'll find some Drain Materia, while further up the road on your left, in an alcove is aChocobo Armlet.

Central Tunnel - Level 6

At the top of this road, just as mentioned by the 3rd class SOLDIER operative who intercepted you earlier, you can hit the switch on the left side of the gigantic door there to proceed. However, when you first examine the switch, you'll be assailed by another group of enemies. Once they're dispatched, you'll be free to head to the switch once more. This time, upon examination the door will open. Hollander is found on the other side, but he runs off, leaving a newly-designed tank to deal with you.

This battle can be a real nuisance, not because the General's Tank is anything extraordinary, but because it's so resilient to attack. The key to destroying it is understanding its weakness - lightning-based magic. As you'll no doubt notice when fighting it, the General's Tank doesn't take much damage from physical attacks. Even if you flank it, which is easy because it's so slow moving (especially when it dedicates itself to a certain attack), damage will be minimal. Breaking out lightning-based magic will damage it five times more than a regular attack. That's the bottom line.

You won't only be dealing with the General's Tank here, however. His five Support Machines will fly around, using their weak electricity attacks. They can rely on the bomb-like potency of their self-destruct attack, however, so dispatch them quickly (keep in mind that the General's Tank can revive these foes by way of the Eject! attack). The General's Tank itself will rely on two primary attacks -- the Gatling Gun and the 203mm Cannon. The latter is stronger, but since it spams this attack with regularity, flanking this foe is easy if you insist on using physical attacks. Oh, and any remaining Support Machines will be killed once the General's Tank is gone.

After the fight, some friendly faces will show up on the scene, Tseng included. Zack must proceed onward to try and catch up with Hollander, so there's no time to waste. Feel free to talk to anyone around you, as there are many friendly faces in the area. You should be sure to talk to Cloud, as well, so that a short cutscene ensues. This will add a new memory event in Cloud's D.M.W. Thereafter, head to the nearby save point, where you can save your game and catch up on some e-mails that have been stacking up throughout this chapter. Then, when you're ready, head forward from the save point to the switch on the wall.

Upper Junon

Now this area is a little different. In fact, it plays a little bit like, say, Chrono Trigger, in that the enemy parties you have to engage can be seen on the map, represented by a lone foe of the enemy party in question. As far as we can tell, twenty-eight total enemies must be eliminated here before you can proceed. This doesn't mean twenty-eight parties. It means twenty-eight enemies. It could be twelve parties you fight, or ten. Regardless, you'll be fighting two kinds of enemies -- powerful Crazy Saws, and the significantly weaker Metal Saucers. If you meet a party with both types of foes, be sure to clear the lesser foes first. Lightning-based magic works well on both enemies if you are in a pinch.

Run into the next area. There are no enemies here, nor are there any treasures to grab. There is a save point, however, the final one in this chapter. Be sure to utilize it, because as you head forward through the gates from the save point, you'll encounter the chapter's primary boss.

Boss Battle - Guard Scorpion

HP	MP	STEAL	DROP
49180	0	Shinra Beta	Vital Slash

The area in which you fight the Guard Scorpion is tight. Since the enemy is so huge, you'll be further limited as to where you can maneuver your character. Making matters worse, the Guard Scorpion has plenty of hit points, so this battle is going to last a while, even if you're higher-leveled than you should be. He has two primary special attacks that he'll use with regularity. One is the EM Field attack that a lot of foes of his kind employ, and since you'll be battling in tight quarters, it's better to block it than to try to avoid it. The other is the Type-98 Cannon, an easily-dodged shotgun attack. He does employ a third special attack, however, one that is completely unavoidable and is pre-empted, by another special move.

If the Guard Scorpion begins to employ his Target Search, you want to dodge it at all costs. If it hits you, his unavoidable Tail Laser attack will decimate your health. Because of this, stay healed and keep on your toes so you can dodge any incoming attacks, and keep attacking the foe, preferably from behind, to whittle away at his substantial hit points. Lightning-based magic works well here, too, but casting time is the downside to trying to use it too often. Stick to physical attacks.

Part 07: The End of Genesis?

Midgar

When you regain control after all those cut-scenes, save your game and leave the Church. Get rid of the three Gun Bull Heads outside. Now you have to gather the materials to build a flower wagon for Aerith.

Don't forget to talk to the little girl by the east exit of the slums street. This will unlock Mission 2-1-4 in the Missions menu. Also, talk to the Silver Elite member in the Park to get a new e-mail from the fan club.

- Tools: Check one of the shiny objects on the ground outside the church to find some Used Tools.

- Wood: Examine wood planks at northeast corner of the market. Tell the carpenter to name his bar "Seventh Heaven". He will then give you some Old Lumber.

- Wheels: Talk to the man standing by the pickup in Loveless Avenue. He will give you his valued Worn Tires.

As for the instructions, head back to the Church Entrance and check the shiny object on the ground. You will receive the How to Build a Wagon book. Go into the church and talk to Aerith to start building the first wagon.

Shinra Building

Enter the briefing room on the Soldier Floor and check the supply pods to get a Sprint Shoes. Go on to the entrance, and speak to the receptionist in brown suit at the Information Center. She is the chairwoman of the new Zack fan club. Cissnei told you about this back at Junon.

Now head to the upper level of the Building Entrance, and talk to the Infantryman hanging around to the east of the hallway. This will unlock Mission 2-1-5. Proceed to the Exhibit Room afterwards. There, speak to the researcher standing in front of the map display. This will unlock Mission 2-1-6. Clear the mission and talk to the researcher again for some story events, then you will receive the Mythril Tools.

Sector 8 - Fountain

If you joined Angeal's and Genesis's fan clubs early on in the game, talk to the Genesis Fan here. It turns out that the club is running low on funds, so go on and suggest that they "merge with a rich fan club". Now head to Loveless Avenue and speak to the other Genesis Fan, who is part of the Loveless Study Group (you need to have joined this club before too).

Return to the Fountain and speak to the Genesis Fan again. This ensures that you continue receiving mails from the Red Leather fan club.

Next, talk to the boy who is running around. He says his mom is missing. So head over to the Sector 1 Platform and talk to the woman there. Select the 2nd option as your response. She should go back to where her son is now. This should keep the Keepers of Honor fan club going.

Sector 5 Slums

Go into the Church and approach Aerith for some cut-scenes. When you regain control at the Shinra Building, head for the elevator, and when prompted for a response, pick the second option. Make your way back to the Church and talk to Aerith, and build another flower wagon for her.

- Craftsman Monthly: Clear mission 1-2-6 and talk to the Shinra Captain in Loveless Avenue.

- Premium Tires: Clear mission 7-1-6 and speak to the Soldier 3rd Class in the Shinra Building Briefing Room.

- Walnut Wood: Complete the Wutai Spies mini-game.

- Mythril Tools: Clear missions 2-1-1 to 2-1-6 and talk to the researcher in the Shinra Building Exhibit Room.

This will trigger some more story events with Aerith. After that, talk to her again to build one last flower wagon for her. You need to have beaten all the opponents for the squats mini-game in the Training Room.

Go back to the Shinra Building, and talk to Kunsel in the SOLDIER Floor. Pick the first option. Take note that this is the last time you will be in Midgar, so make sure that you're really ready before you go.

Part 08: Departure

Nibelheim

When you regain control after the short cut-scene and the dialogue with Tifa, talk to Sephiroth them to Cloud outside the Inn. After that, go speak to the boy near the east exit to play the "Seven Wonders of Nibelheim" mini-game. Just talk to the boy after solving a mystery to do the next one.

- 1st Wonder: Climb up the water tank at the center of the area, to find the Phoenix Materia in the water.

- 2nd Wonder: Go inside the Inn, up to 2F, and into the bed room. Have a look at the painting of the girl in black. Leave the room and go back in. Check the painting again and the girl should be gone. Now go back downstairs, and you should see the clerk walking around. Follow him upstairs and into the bed room. He will give you 2000 Gil.

- 3rd Wonder: Head for the town outskirts and take the north exit toward Mt. Nibel Trail. There, make your way to the east dead end, and run around to initiate some random encounters. You should meet some Gray Bombs and Touchy Bombs here. Keep defeating these enemies until they drop some Gold Shards. You'll get a Safety Bit.

- 4th Wonder: Go to the Shinra Manor, which is located west of the town outskirts. Head to 2F then west at the hallway. Enter the upper room. Examine the note on the floor for your hint on the safe combination. Peek into the keyholes of the locked doors to find your numbers.

1. Digit 1: The number of books that are not in the shelf.

2. Digit 2: The number of monsters in one of the locked rooms on 1F.

3. Digit 3: The total number of apple juice and dumbapples.

4. Digit 4: The number of chairs in one of the locked rooms on 1F.

Once you open the safe, a Cactuar will come out and you will get a mastered Vital Slash Materia inside. You won't be able to work on the 5th wonder yet. So go back to 2F of the Inn and speak to Sephiroth.

Mount Nibel

At the Reactor Entrance, pick up a White Cape from the chest nearby. Save your game and head west towards the Mountain Trail. There, head for the east dead end for a Hi-Potion, HP Stone, and Elixir. Head back south to Nibelheim. When you regain control after the story events, head for Shinra Manor, which is located to the west of Nibelheim Outskirts. But go for the east exit first and grab an Ether from the treasure chest there.

Shinra Manor

Save your game, go upstairs, and head east at the hallway. Enter the upper right room and check the stone wall to access the basement. Pick up a Soma from the chest and descend the ladder to the lower level.

- 5th Wonder: Defeat the Sahagin enemies to get the Coffin Keys. Then enter the southeast room and use the key on the right coffin.

Open the treasure chest for a Talisman. Go back outside and head for the southwest room and grab the X-Potion from the chest. Now leave that room and enter the Basement Facility to the south. When you regain control after the story events, leave the library and pick up the Elixir.

Nibelheim

6th Wonder: Talk to the boy outside the burning house and agree to save his mom. You won't see where you're going here. Experiment with the directions until you find the way up. Talk to the mom, feel your way back down and out of the store. The boy gives an ATK UP++ Materia.

Have a look around the area here to find a chest with a Fire Ring in it. After that, head for the exit and make your way to the Reactor Entrance. Save your game there. Go inside for some scenes and a boss fight.

Boss Battle - Sephiroth

HP	MP	STEAL	DROP
52820	9999	N/A	N/A

HP	MP	STEAL	DROP
31900	9999	N/A	N/A

A battle with Sephiroth. This should bring back some memories, eh? This battle is manageable, and if you're high-leveled, you'll have an even easier time expelling Sephiroth in this battle. However, he has a special technique and three special attacks that you should know about -- those in addition to his normal multi-swipe attack that's actually surprisingly weak. Sephiroth can teleport around. That's his special skill. This works to his advantage because you'll often commit yourself to a combo or spell that will miss him as he disappears, leaving you vulnerable if he happens to reappear behind you. He can also use the very same Octaslash attack that you can use via his skill in your own DMW. However, it's his weakest special attack. The ones you want to watch out for follow. Draw Slash is a powerful attack that can thrust you back with great force while shaving a couple thousand HP from your meter. If he uses it, try to run away from him, since if he's far enough away, he'll miss. The real killer is his Heartless Angel attack. This attack, if it connects, will diminish your HP all the way to 1! If used, immediately heal, because the next attack will end the battle. Otherwise, you should be well-prepared for this rather lackluster battle. We know -- it's Sephiroth, and you expected more.

This battle with Sephiroth is arguably easier than the last one, but there's a major catch to this battle. The catch is that you're fighting on a thin platform, and if Sephiroth manages to push you to the very end of the platform, you'll die automatically. Because of this, all-out aggressive tactics are absolutely, positively necessary here in order to succeed. Stay close to Sephiroth no matter what, remembering that you can interrupt each and every one of his attacks (except for the weak Octaslash) simply by striking him before he gets the attack out. This goes for the Heartless Angel and the ever-dangerous Draw Slash, the latter of which can easily push you over the edge if you're not careful. Go for broke here - he has less hit points so as long as you stay away from the edge, you're clear.

Part 09: See You Soon

Nibelheim

At the Shinra Manor Basement Facility, "talk" to the scientist to get the Dresser Key. You can also check the floor to find some of the scientist's notes and read them. Go into the library and grab 10000 Gil from the chest. Exit back out to the Underground Cave, and head up to the Manor. Zack will automatically go back to get Cloud each time you try to leave.

At the Manor, head down to the first floor. Pick up a Shinra Beta from the treasure chest. Leave the Manor and make your way to the east exit towards Nibelheim Defeat all the Shinra infantrymen before they manage to drag Cloud out to the exit. Check distance from the bottom counter.

- 7th Wonder: If you managed to save the boy's mother from the fire earlier, you will receive an email from him saying that he left you a gift somewhere in the village. Head east at the village outskirts, and pick up the Wall Materia next to the fence of one of the houses.

Shinra Manor

Now you must find some clothes for Cloud to change into. So head into the bottom room west of the hallway. Use the Dresser Key to unlock the closet. You should get 5000 Gil and a SOLDIER Outfit in there. Go back to Cloud's room and talk to him. Defeat all the infantrymen outside.

Nibel Plains

Make your way to the west end of the plains. Pick up the sniper rifles you find along the way, and use it to destroy the Gun Bull Heads patrolling the area. Aim for the upper part of the machines, or the red eye at the top to score instant kills. You can also aim for the other parts and shoot them repeatedly until you destroy them. They will flee if you take too long.

You can then use the kill points you accumulated to purchase upgrades for the rifle. The machines you destroy during combat also count as kills. The content of the treasure at the end of the path will depend on how well you did in the sniping mini-game. That is if you managed to keep your total Fled Points (FP) to a minimum. Possible rewards are listed below:

- 0 FP: Dragon Armlet, Gravity, Dash, Thundaga.

- 01-02 FP: Gravity, Thundaga, Dash.

- 03-05 FP: Thundaga, Dash.

- 06-10 FP: Thundaga

Save your game and continue towards the dead end for a boss battle.

Boss Battle - G Eliminator

HP	MP	STEAL	DROP
65300	999	Iron Bangle	Blast Wave

The G Eliminator is yet another of the many copies of Genesis that seem to want to kill you no matter what. This foe doesn't have a vast array of attacks -- in fact, he'll cast Firaga and Thundaga almost exclusively -- but he does pack a powerful punch, necessitating your regular use of healing spells to combat lost hit points. Additionally, G Eliminator can (and will) swipe at you for 1,000+ hit points in damage for each hit, and he can't be staggered with your own attacks, meaning you'll be susceptible to counter-attacks throughout the entire battle. The good news is that his magic attacks, especially Thundaga, are easy to dodge, and when he commits himself to a spell, he'll leave his flank open, so make sure to get in there with due haste and inflict some critical damage when you can. Then, back away, so that he can't retaliate with his powerful physical attacks. He does have one special attack worth mentioning, called Stranglehold. This can't be dodged, but is weaker than the rest of Eliminator's attacks.

Gongaga

Walk to the northeast corner of the area and talk to the man there. Now you should see treasure chests blocked by fences or on top of barrels. Examine the "rubble" and bust through them. You will get 6000 Gil and a Hypno Crown. Beat the monsters in the rattling treasure chests to get an Osmoga Materia and a Zeio Nut. Go north to the outskirts of town.

Gongaga Outskirts

Pick up a Remedy from the treasure chest and save your game. Move south for a scene. When you regain control, check the small "alley" going north to the left of the save point for another chest with a Headband in it. Turn back southeast and open one more chest along the way, to get the Research Dept. QMC+ (Shop). Exit southeast towards the Hills.

Follow the path here and pick up a Remedy and Elixir along the way. When you reach the top, defeat the enemies for a cut-scene. You can also play a minigame at the waterfalls. To play it, you must first fight 7 random battles by running around the area, then try to head for the exit.

In this minigame, you need to collect as many treasure chests as you can within approximately a minute or so. You can grab a chest by running up to it. Avoid getting hit by the monsters by getting onto dry land. If you get incapacitated, press O repeatedly to recover. Possible rewards below:

- 10+ Chests: Hi-Potion, X-Potion, Elixir, Goblin Punch.

- 08 - 09 Chests: Hi-Potion, X-Potion, Elixir.

- 05 - 07 Chests: Hi-Potion, X-Potion.

- 01 - 04 Chests: Hi-Potion.

Rush back to the Abandoned Mako Reactor next for a boss battle.

Boss Battle - Hollander

HP	MP	STEAL	DROP
98540	156	Dark Matter	Status Ward

Once again, start off by casting Barrier and MBarrier then move in and begin bashing him. Hollander's Deathly Breath attack causes Poison, Silence, Curse, and nullifies your status enhancements. Try to avoid getting hit by it as much as you can. But if it connects, use a Remedy to remove the status effects. Hollander will also summon a bunch of Land Worms, which can cause Stop. Also, when he says "I'm alright now", he becomes invincible. Wait for the invincibility status to wear off and resume your attacks. He will eventually use his Dimension Missile, which is a gravity-like attack that takes away 75% of your HP so heal!

Part 10: Heroes

Banora

Proceed forward and descend into the lifestream pit, where you must keep going to eventually reach a new area, the Depths of Judgement.

Depths of Judgement

Move forward and open the treasure chest to get the Light Materia. Follow the path down to the lower level and save your game. From here, head east then north up the slope. The chest contains the Heaven Materia.

Come back down and go through the opening on the rockface nearby. Grab the Ground Materia inside then head back out. Make your way eastward, then around west at the bottom path to find another chest with the Star Materia. Turn back and take the south exit to Lake of Oblivion.

Lake Oblivion

Open the nearby treasure chest to get the Life Materia. Next proceed to the middle-left portion of the area to find another chest with the Being Materia. Then head for the top-right section to find the chest containing the last goddess materia, the Sabbath Materia. Save your game now.

Examine the lifestream pools in the area, and defeat the enemies that appear. In order to fight these enemies, you must first read all of the LOVELESS tablets that are scattered in the entire dungeon. There are five of these pools here. Find them all and the path leading to the Cage of Binding will appear. When it does, head north and go through the new exit.

Cage of Binding

Trigger some random enemy encounter and defeat some Nightmares to get the Goddess Base Key and the Goddess Sacral Key. Turn the valve on cell #1 to open it and get a River Chocobo Armlet. Use the keys you found to unlock the goddess gate. In the next room, open cell #4; grab the Elixir. Move on towards cell #5 and grab a Graviga Materia here. Run around, find a Mover for the Goddess Solar Key.

In the next room, open cell #9 and go through the hole in the wall. You should emerge within cell #8. Take the Dispel Blade. Go back through the hole and out of cell #9. Kill Death Machines to get the Goddess Throat Key. Unlock the next goddess gate. Open cell #16 and go through the hole in the wall to access cell #15. Grab the Laboratory Key. Go back and out of cell #16. Open cell #17, pick up the Gris-Gris Bag.

Ignore the goddess gate up ahead for now. Instead run around along the center path to the right until you encounter a Mover enemy. Kill it to get the Goddess Heart Key. Use that to unlock the east goddess gate. Open cell #13 and get a Phoenix Down inside. Next go unlock the door next to cell #11 using the Laboratory Key. Read the documents on the tables. After that, make your way back to the save point in cell #17 and save your game. Then go unlock the other goddess gate nearby and go on through.

Howling Fang

Run around until you encounter some Evil Eye enemies. Kill them to get the Goddess Third Eye Key. Go on and open cell #19 then cell #20. Get a Mag Up++ Materia from the chest. Next open cell #23 for a Silver Armlet. After that, go through the hole in the wall of cell #22.

You should end up at cell #29. Again, run around until you meet a tank enemy. Kill it to get the Goddess Crown Key. Use that to unlock the nearby goddess gate. Grab the Iron Bars Key inside. Now go back and head through the hole in the wall of cell #27 to access cell #18. Collect an HP Up++ and Atk Up+ Materia from the pair of treasure chests.

Go back and out of cell #27. Proceed north along the center path and unlock the goddess gate. Continue further up, then go open cell #32 and exit out to cell #36. Save your game and use the Iron Bars Key to open the cage. Defeat the Behemoth King to get the Goddess Wing Key. Use that to open the goddess gate up ahead. Proceed to the next area.

Portal of Severance

Ride the elevator down to the lower level. Examine the pedestal and set all seven goddess materia on it to open the gate leading to the final boss chamber. Save your game and go through the gate when you're ready. You will be treated to some cut-scenes, followed by a boss battle.

Boss Battle - Genesis Avatar

HP	MP	STEAL	DROP
600000	2301	N/A	N/A

The battle with Genesis Avatar is similar to your run in(s) with Fury Bahamut throughout the game (plural if you've fought him in optional missions in addition to your run-in with him throughout the regular course of the game). It's similar in that the enemy isn't on the field of battle with you, but rather stands to the side of it and hovers over it with his massive size. This isn't a battle of brawn and strength, but rather a battle of longevity. As you go through this battle, you'll see just what we mean. You won't be attacking the foe himself, but rather the materia on his sword. He sticks his sword in the ground and keeps it there as he summons enemies to the field of battle to help him in the form of G Shadow Scythes (physical attackers) and G Shadow Mages (magical attackers).

So, you'll need to strike at his sword as much as you can when it's in the ground to damage him while fending off his minions. It's not as easy as it sounds, because these foes will crowd you and, in addition to using physical attacks, will cast plenty of magic (Blizzaga, Firaga, et cetera) to stymie your advance. Genesis Avatar himself can cast HP, MP and AP-draining magic, as well as use Shadow Flare (easily avoidable), Flare (unavoidable), and Purgatorial Wave (devastatingly unavoidable). The key here is to stay well-healed, pray for some good DMW help, and to take your time. This battle will take a while whether or not you rush, but rushing will only catalyze your demise. Do as much as you can when you can, and then take a breather. Repeat the process for a hard fought victory.

Watch the scenes and prepare for another battle boss battle.

Boss Battle - Genesis

HP	MP	STEAL	DROP
99999	9999	N/A	N/A

his battle with Genesis is it, but strangely, it's not that hard of a battle. Genesis is a strong, quick fighter, and getting off multiple hits on him in sequence without being hit yourself is unlikely. So, you'll need to chip away at his health while keeping your own health up in response to his varying attacks. Thankfully, he doesn't have nearly the hit points his previous monstrous version did, so you don't have much to worry about. In fact, with one exception, all of his attacks are avoidable and their affects can be negated with a quick Cura spell. Here's what to expect attack-wise from Genesis. Flash, Homing, and Magic Sword hit multiple times.

One or more of the hits can be blocked or dodged all together. Twister Strike and Dancing Sword are melee attacks that he'll conduct when he's close by -- dodging these attacks is likely your best bet. And then, there's Apocalypse. This attack is unavoidable, but you'll likely recognize it from your own DMW, since when three Genesis faces come up on the DMW, you'll use the same attack. Even though it's unavoidable, it happens to be a weak attack. So no worries here. In fact, no worries with this fight at all.

Watch the ending cut-scenes. You will soon be controlling Zack again.

Final Battle - Shinra Army

Well this is a story event so you can't really die here. But still there are so many infantrymen, plus choppers that fire missiles at you. You can only attack the soldiers on the ground. Since you can't really get rid of everyone, so just try to kill off as many enemies as you can.

When the last ending FMV sequence ends, you will be given a chance to save your game. Do so, then load that save to play in New game +. In this mode, all equipment (materia and accessories) you collected, Zack's level, and the percentage of each DMW entry from previous playthroughs will be carried over. While mission progress and DMW entries are reset.

MISSIONS

01-01: Shinra Basic Training

Mission 1-1-1 Shinra's Basic Training

- **Enemies:** None.
- **Objective Party:** Sentry (x8)
- **Prize:** Elixir
- **Information:** "This is a simulated battle against infantrymen. The difficulty level is set low, so it should pose no problem for a SOLDIER operative. Relax and enjoy the training."
- **Notes:** This is the first mission in the game, and it's a mandatory one. Thankfully, it's extremely simplistic and will require nothing more than some sword hacking and slashing.

01-02: Peacekeeping Troops

Mission 1-2-1: Challenge from Security

- **Enemies:** Storm Trooper
- **Objective Party:** Storm Trooper (x4)
- **Prize:** Shinra Alpha
- **Information:** "Members of the Security Department have requested a joint training session with SOLDIER. Some of them seem to regard SOLDIER with a passionate sense of rivalry. It's only a training session, but don't take it lightly."
- **Notes:** From the outset, head forward and then swing left at the first opportunity (going forward will result in meeting a dead end). You'll be fighting Storm Troopers here, who are week gun-toting foes who like to throw grenades (so dodge them before they explode!) Go down the stairs and take your *second* left. Go down the stairs to the last room and turn around to find an **X-Potion** in a chest. Then, backtrack to the previous corridor and head down to the end of it (so that there's only a barrier in between you and the end of the mission). A **Remedy** can be found in a nearby chest. With that in hand, swing down the only remaining unexplored corridor, where the objective party can be found. Four Storm Troopers should hardly be a challenge for you.

Mission 1-2-2: Second Challenge

- **Enemies:** Storm Trooper, Red Saucer
- **Objective Party:** Corporal, Red Saucer (x3)
- **Prize:** Silence Materia
- **Information:** "Members of the Security Department have requested another joint training session with SOLDIER. They have robots to support them this time. Proceed with caution."
- **Notes:** If you take a look at the map of this area, there simply isn't anywhere to deviate. You can head directly forward to the objective party, fighting random enemies along the way. Be sure to grab the **X-Potion** from the treasure chest en route, as well. The objective party is made up of a Corporal (a mildly stronger version of a Storm Trooper) and three Red Saucers. This should be absolutely no problem for you whatsoever.

Mission 1-2-3: Third Challenge

- **Enemies:** Storm Trooper, Corporal, Red Saucer

- **Objective Party:** Corporal (x2), Red Saucer (x2)
- **Prize:** Four Slots
- **Information:** "Members of the Security Department have requested yet another joint training session with SOLDIER. A statement from them reads: "We were holding back in the previous sessions." They are desperate and may do anything to save face. Be careful."
- **Notes:** Before running forward down the path, turn around and go in the other direction. You'll ultimately be led to a dead end, but an **Elixir** can be found here. Once you've grabbed it, head back to the starting point and continue down the pathway ahead. When you get to a fork, where you can go left or right, go left. Ignore the pathway you come across on your right and proceed forward to grab a **Hi-Potion** With it in hand, you can then proceed rightward and leftward to the objective party, made up of two Corporals and two Red Saucers. Again, nothing you can't handle.

Mission 1-2-4: Getting Serious

- **Enemies:** Storm Trooper, Corporal, Red Saucer
- **Objective Party:** Corporal (x4)
- **Prize:** Force Bracelet
- **Information:** "The persistent members of the Security Department have sent SOLDIER another challenge to a joint training session. Making excuses, they claim the difference in budget between the departments to be the reason for their losses. Go show them exactly why we are combat experts."
- **Notes:** This area is one giant circle, but it's best to take the right path around it. This will run you into a **Soma** in a chest on your right as you go around the circle. When you finally see the objective party waiting for you, be sure to grab the chest containing a **Hi-Potion** on your left before approaching them. The enemy party here is made up of four Corporals. That's right -- pushovers. So no worries.

Mission 1-2-5: Armed Challenge

- **Enemies:** Corporal, Red Saucer, Sweeper+
- **Objective Party:** Sweeper+ (x2)
- **Prize:** Ice Armlet
- **Information:** "Members of the Security Department have sent SOLDIER yet another challenge to a joint training session. It seems they have succeeded in securing funds, and have new weapons at their disposal. We in SOLDIER never blame a loss on the budget. Win the session and teach them the meaning of dignity."
- **Notes:** Head forward along the pathway before you, and swing right along with it. When you get the option to head left towards the waiting enemy party, resist the urge for the time being and head right instead. This linear pathway will lead to a dead end ultimately, but you'll be able to find a **Hi-Potion** and a **Remedy** by exploring down there. After grabbing both items, you can then backtrack to the enemy party's location (be sure to grab the **Potion** en route). The enemy party is made up of two Sweeper+ robotic foes, who you actually face en route to them in the first place. They are far more powerful than anything else you've faced in this string of missions, but again, nothing too crazy. Their slow movements make them prime targets for critical attacks from behind.

Mission 1-2-6: Last Challenge

- **Enemies:** Flying Machine, Corporal, Sweeper+
- **Objective Party:** Arachno
- **Prize:** Fat Chocobo Feather
- **Information:** "Members of the Security Department, on a losing streak, have yet again challenged SOLDIER to a joint training session. They have used up their entire budget on this one. We know we've had too many of these, but this one is sure to be the last. Savor it for what it is."

- **Notes:** The pathway here is completely linear, so getting lost is somewhat of an impossibility. Head south, and then swing east along with the pathway. As the path swings forward for the last time, you'll find the two items available here -- an **Elixir** and a **Hi-Potion** (to find the latter item, you'll need to turn around, as it's against a door jam you come through). You'll also be fighting new enemies here called Flying Machines, who are much more robust and combat-worthy than anything else you've seen in this chain of missions. When you finally reach the objective party, you'll find that it's nothing you've ever seen. It's an Arachno, a giant spider-like creature. This robotic enemy has two attacks of notice. It's Shinra Type 100 Cannon is a devastating but easy-to-dodge attack, while its Super EM Field is an attack used to light up the area around it. The latter is tougher to dodge, especially because you'll be up close to the foe in order to damage him. Thankfully, the enemy is relatively slow-moving, so getting behind him to attack him for critical damage is somewhat easy. It's necessary, too, since the foe has plenty of HP to back up his attack power.

01-03: Weapons Development

Mission 1-3: Weapons Development

Mission 1-3-1: Next-Generation Weapons

- **Enemies:** Sweeper+, Guard Fang
- **Objective Party:** Guard Fang (x3)
- **Prize:** Assault Twister Materia
- **Information:** "After vanishing from Wutai, Genesis has formed his own army and commenced an attack on Shinra troops. Shinra is developing new weapons to counter the emerging threat. We want you to participate in testing these weapons."
- **Notes:** If you take a look at this map, it's a wide-open field. What's more, there doesn't appear to be any treasure anywhere on the map, so you can make straight for the objective party at your convenience (they're waiting for you at the northeast edge of the map). The party is made up of three Guard Fangs, foes you can actually find here on the map regularly. However, apart from their pesky Tentacle attacks, they are nothing to worry about at all. They are fast-moving, but that's about it.

Mission 1-3-2: New Mechanical Weapons

- **Enemies:** Guard Fang, Red Saucer II
- **Objective Party:** Needle Machine
- **Prize:** Cura Materia
- **Information:** "The Shinra weapons that vanished with Genesis reappeared in his forces' hands. To counter them, we have started developing new and improved weapons. We ask for your support in testing this enhanced gear."
- **Notes:** Thankfully, this area requires very little exploration. There are two items to find as you go forward, however. An **Elixir** can be found on your left, and then further up on your right, you can find an **X-Potion**. These white treasure chests are mixed up with debris, however, so you might have to get to them via a little bit of exploration. When you approach the objective party, you'll find that it's a mechanical device known as a Needle Machine. This foe has one primary attack which can be quite devastating. It's called Holy Lance, and it should be dodged at all costs, because it can do 1,500 HP in damage to even well-leveled players.

Mission 1-3-3: To Quash Genesis's Forces

- **Enemies:** Launcher Machine, Chain Machine

- **Objective Party:** Red Saucer II, Chain Machine
- **Prize:** Thundaga Materia
- **Information:** "The New Weapons Group, dedicated to developing more powerful weapons, has obtained extensive operations data on the weapons used by Genesis's forces. They have succeeded in developing new weapons that should overwhelm their current arsenal. We want you to participate in testing these weapons."
- **Notes:** You'll start out at the far south end of a pathway. This pathway will wind up in a linear fashion until you have the opportunity to go right to meet up with the objective party. Before doing so, head forward to the dead end, where you can find **Blizzaga Materia** in the treasure chest there. A quick word on the enemies here, too. You will find Launcher and Chain Machines, and both are forces to be reckoned with. Launcher Machine's Missile attack is especially devastating. Be sure to block or dodge when he launches those suckers. The enemy party is made up of a Red Saucer II (a more powerful version of Red Saucer) and the aforementioned Chain Machine. Hey -- at least it's not a Launcher Machine you're dealing with.

Mission 1-3-4: Experiments Gone Wrong

- **Enemies:** Guard Fang, Launcher Machine, Chain Machine
- **Objective Party:** Needle Machine
- **Prize:** River Chocobo Armlet
- **Information:** "Hastily-developed weapons designed to fight Genesis have gone berserk. The testing site is closed off, so there is no concern of damages spreading outside, but we must bring the situation under control. Destroy all machines inside the testing area."
- **Notes:** Ahead of you as you begin, you can either head left or right. While the objective party is located down the corridor to your right, you should first head left. There's a dead end there, but there's also a **Soma** for you to acquire. Once you've added it to your inventory, run back down the path in the other direction, doing battle with difficult enemies we've already faced before. The objective party, once reached, will be another Needle Machine, which you should have faced before. Remember -- its Holy Lance attack should be dodged at all costs.

Mission 1-3-5: Robots in the City

- **Enemies:** Red Saucer II, Bee Saucer II, Drill Machine
- **Objective Party:** Drill Machine, Red Saucer II (x2)
- **Prize:** Graviga Materia
- **Information:** "New weapons have been developed to counter the elusive Genesis copies in the city. Your cooperation is needed in the testing area for us to obtain combat data for defending Midgar."
- **Notes:** This is yet another area that requires very little exploration. All you have to do is head forward along the wide pathway. There are two items to find here, but you'll find neither until you've neared the objective party's location. You can find a **Mountain Chocobo Armlet** on your left, and further up the path, nearer the enemy party's location, a **Hi-Potion** can be acquired. A word on the enemies here known as Red Saucer II. These foes are annoying not because of any other reason but their ability to cast Wall on themselves and their fellow party members. This increases defense and makes casting spells on enemies a no-no. When you fight the objective party, therefore, you'll want to concentrate on taking them out first. The Drill Machine is annoying enough as it is without having to worry about increased defense!

Mission 1-3-6: A Director's Request

- **Enemies:** Proto Power Head
- **Objective Party:** Escort Head, Proto Power Head (x2)
- **Prize:** Crystal Bracelet

- **Information:** "We have been asked by Director Scarlet at the Arms Development Department to test new weapons. This is a new version of an unmanned weapon currently in use, and we must collect as much combat data as possible. Destroy all machines within the battle area."
- **Notes:** The foes you'll be facing here are dangerous, so you'll want to keep a careful eye on your health going forward. Proto Power Heads are just about the only foes you'll face, and they have devastating attacks that can do 1,500 HP of damage to a level 25 Zack. Thankfully, the pathway to the objective party is a one-way street, so there's little exploration that needs to be done. Simply follow the linear path to its ultimate conclusion (and be absolutely sure to grab the **Curaga Materia** from the treasure chest en route). The objective party is a difficult one. Two Proto Power Heads will accompany an Escort Head, and they're all annoying. Flanking them together for critical damage on more than one target at a time is your best bet.

02-01: Monsters in Midgar

Mission 2-1-4: Defend the Slums

Enemies: Fly Eye, Raijincho, Grashtrike
Objective Party: Raijincho (x3)
Prize: Fire Ring
Information: "Residents of the slums have decided to take matters into their own hands to fight the monsters. Hurry there and eliminate the monsters before any of the slum residents are hurt."
Notes: This mission will bring you to a wide open field, but as far as we can tell, there are no items to find anywhere in this vast terrain. That's a good thing, since running around excessively will result in numerous random battles with run-of-the-mill enemies found here -- Fly Eyes and Raijinchos of the airborne variety, and small ground-dwelling snakes called Grashtrikes. The objective party, a group of three Raijinchos, is located in the far corner of the area from where you start, so head straight there to begin the battle. The only attack they have of any consequence is a lightning-based attack that can be easily dodged. You'll likely run into this mission after you've been playing for a while, however, so you should be plenty-leveled for this battle.

02-02: Monster Reports

Mission 2-2-1: Slums of Midgar

Enemies: Hedgehog Pie, Worm
Objective Party: Hedgehog Pie (x2), Worm (x2)
Prize: Assault Twister Materia
Information: "This is a battle with monsters who claim the slums of lower Midgar as their turf. There actually is little strength to them; perhaps you can use them to work out your tactics for fighting against monsters."
Notes: By the time this mission unlocks itself, you'll be more prepared than needed to take on the enemies here. What's more, the area *seems* vast, but isn't so at all. Because of this fact, this should be a really quick endeavor. Simply go forward towards the already-visible enemy party, grabbing a **Star Pendant** from the treasure chest on your left en route. The enemy party is made up of two Hedgehog Pies and two Worms, and both are easily slain. The Worms use their String attack often, which can stun you, so dodge it if it's flying your way!

03-01: Genesis's Forces

Mission 3-1-1: Foes on the Waterfront

- **Enemies:** Guard Hound, G Assassin
- **Objective Party:** Blood Taste (x2), G Assassin
- **Prize:** Bronze Bangle
- **Information:** "The coast guard has spotted Genesis troops, so they're likely to have an outpost near the coast. Head there and vanquish the enemy!"
- **Notes:** No matter when you choose to undertake this mission once it's available to you, it's going to be an easy endeavor. The mission will start you out in front of the objective party, but resist the allure of running straight for them. Instead, run in the opposite direction in the only other way you can go (take a look at your map). At the end of the other corridor, you'll find an **X-Potion** on the left side in a chest. Grab it, then backtrack to where you started out and run toward the objective party. Before getting close enough to engage, however, be sure to check the tall grass on the right for a **Potion**. The enemy party is a pushover - a G Assassin (which should be a one or two-hit kill for you) and two Blood Tastes, which are mildly stronger versions of the Guard Hounds you'll fight in random battles here. Easy, easy.

Mission 3-1-2: Massive Machines

Enemies: Heli Gunner, G Assassin
- **Objective Party:** Guard Spider
- **Prize:** Iron Bangle
- **Information:** "We have received reports of Genesis troops hiding large-scale weapons in the caves. Destroy them and stop their advance."
- **Notes:** You'll find yourself in a vast pathway leading forward, with the objective party sitting there waiting for you. There's simply no place to deviate on this map, so head forward. There will be a **Remedy** in a chest on your left as you proceed forward (Heli Gunners and weak G Assassins will be all you have to worry about here, so no worries). Proceed to the battle with the Guard Spider, who is a simplistic enemy more daunting in looks than anything else. He can be felled with regular attacks rather easily, although getting behind him to deal critical blows can be a bit of a nuisance with his speed.

Mission 3-1-3: Eliminate the Copies

- **Enemies:** Red Saucer, Sweeper, G Avenger, Kactuar
- **Objective Party:** G Avenger (x2), G Eraser
- **Prize:** AP Up Materia
- **Information:** "Genesis troops have been ID'd by scouts on their way to the wasteland. Vanquish this core group and stop the enemy from moving in!"
- **Notes:** From the outset, head forward, being sure to open up the treasure chest that's in your path to find a **Wrist Band**. Then, swing rightward with the pathway, where the objective party is located. However, avoid this battle for the time being, swinging leftward along the next path (staying against the wall so as to not accidentally trigger this battle). Ahead on this path is a Kactuar, a famous Final Fantasy character. Do battle with him (he's a pushover) and you'll unlock another series of missions. *Then* backtrack to fight the previous battle we just dodged. This battle will be with two G Avengers and a G Eraser. Make the G Avengers your first target, since they're pushovers. The nightstick and rifle-toting G Eraser is more difficult, however, having myriad attacks. Watch for its ranged rifle attacks, which can be dodged or blocked, and dodge him when he breaks out his Combo Attack, which can be pesky indeed.

Mission 3-1-4: Destroy the Death Machines

- **Enemies:** Red Saucer, Sweeper
- **Objective Party:** Cutter Machine, Pile Machine, Shot Machine (separate battles)
- **Prize:** VIT Up Materia
- **Information:** "We have found a supply depot of Genesis troops! We can slow their momentum by crushing this base. Destroy the three types of Death Machines in their main arsenal and shut down the base!"
- **Notes:** This is a unique mission because there isn't only one objective party to do battle with here, but rather three of them. Each battle is simplistic, but you'll be instantly struck by this fact as you begin the mission, so we thought we'd discuss it instantly. There's also random battles here, but nothing you can't handle. The three objective parties are, in order you'll meet them, a Cutter Machine, a Pile Machine and a Shot Machine. The latter two enemies, though stronger than the Cutter Machine are actually easier to slay because if you continuously hit them without relent, they won't get a chance to unleash their attacks. The Cutter Machine is easy, as well, but dodge his poison attacks! As you head through this linear area, you'll also want to be certain that you grab the **X-Potion** out of the first treasure chest on your left, and a **Hi-Potion** out of the second one you encounter.

Mission 3-1-5: Eliminate the Death Machines

- **Enemies:** Red Saucer, Sweeper
- **Objective Party:** Cutter Machine, Pile Machine, & Shot Machine
- **Prize:** Mythril Gloves
- **Information:** "Genesis's forces are reorganizing. There seems to be no change in their weaponry, but the troops organized around the Death Machines are not to be trifled with. Attack them before they start mobilizing."
- **Notes:** This mission will be short and sweet, with a rather challenging and annoying objective party at the end. It's a completely linear area, so getting lost is impossible. Simply head down the path you begin the mission on, and it will open up into a larger area where the objective party can be instantly seen. Be sure to hug the leftmost wall as you turn into this area, as you will find a treasure chest with an **Ether** in it (veering too far off the path will activate the primary battle). The objective party is made up of the three robotic enemies we fought separately in the previous mission, so having them together is much more of a pain. Depending on when you're undertaking this mission, this may or may not be a massive challenge (we were in the late 20s level-wise). Your best bet is to unleash powerful spells as you run around hacking and slashing. The enemies are aggressive, so they will tend to bunch together, but this also makes dodging multiple attacks an impossibility. Be careful.

Mission 3-1-6: Midgar Defense Operations

- **Enemies:** G Assailant, Bee Saucer, Moth Slasher
- **Objective Party:** G Assailant (x2), G Warrior
- **Prize:** Mystile
- **Information:** "Genesis troops have been sighted in Midgar. The citizenry has been evacuated and the area blocked off. Eradicate the forces before they are able to infiltrate other areas."
- **Notes:** This area is extensive and can be confusing, so follow our instructions closely. Head forward from the area in which you begin, and swing right at the first chance you get. This will allow you to head down a staircase into another corridor (continuing forward in the previous corridor will result in you finding a dead end). Once down the stairs, head forward and swing right again, down the next corridor. You'll reach a dead end here, but you'll find **Thunder Materia** in a treasure chest there. Then, backtrack and continue along the previous path to an identical path further up that you can go right along. A **Remedy** can be found at the end of this path -- simply turn around when you enter the final room of the path, where the treasure chest can be found against the door jam. Rejoin the previous path and continue down, taking your first left. Head up this path and left in the next room -- **Esuna Materia** will be found there. Then, backtrack yet again. If you take a look at the in-game map, there's only one corridor we've yet to explore (but we've been inching towards it all this time). En route, grab the **Soma** from the

treasure chest. The objective party is made up of two lesser G Assailants and a G Warrior. Naturally, you'll want to take out the fodder first (G Assailants) before working on G Warrior. He can attack with Fira, a special attack called Twin Kick, and he can even silence you, so be careful! Either way, though, he's a pushover.

04-01: Pursue the Remnants

Mission 4-1-1: Wutai Units Found

Enemies: Foulander, Wutai Private, Wutai Sergeant
Objective Party: Wutai Sergeant, Foulander (x3)
Prize: Elixir
Information: "We have spotted a detached Wutai army unit on the outskirts of Wutai. We want to prevent any further incidents from them in an already chaotic political environment. Vanquish them before they make a move."
Notes: Run forward from the starting point to acquire an **X-Potion** from the chest on your left. Then run forward and to the left towards the Wutai Sergeant there. As you approach him, he'll attack, along with three Foulanders. Easily take all of the foes out to earn an Elixir for your inventory.

Mission 4-1-2: Anti-SOLDIER Monsters

Enemies: Wutai Private
Objective Party: Vajradhara Wu, Vajradhara Tai
Prize: Bulletproof Vest
Information: "A detached Wutai force has trained monsters to specifically fight SOLDIER operatives. Defeat the anti-SOLDIER creatures and eliminate the remnants."
Notes: Run forward along the linear path. You'll see the monsters you need to fight to your left, but first grab the **X-Potion** from the treasure chest ahead. Then, turn around and run towards the monsters to begin this mission's primary battle. You should be plenty familiar with these enemies, however, because they were in a boss battle in Wutai early in the game. If you beat them then (before this mission was even available), then beating them now shouldn't even remotely be an issue. What's more, you'll get a Bulletproof Vest for your troubles.

Mission 4-1-3: Pursue the Deserters

Enemies: Wutai Soldier Jia, Balo Balo, Wutai Staff Sergeant
Objective Party: Wutai Staff Sergeant, Wutai Soldier Jia (x2)
Prize: Libra Materia
Information: "Fort Tamblin has fallen, but many of their fighters have escaped. They refuse to disarm in an attempt to maintain the resistance. Allowing this to continue would only sow chaos. A swift elimination is in order."
Notes: To find all of the items in this dungeon, you're going to have to do a little searching. However, it's nothing too crazy. Head south from the starting position and bear leftward with the pathway. When you get to a side corridor heading left, take it (though going forward will bring you to this mission's ultimate conclusion). On your left, heading north, you'll find an **X-Potion**, while on the right, further up towards the dead end, you'll find an **Ether**. After grabbing both items, rejoin the previous pathway and continue up towards the enemy waiting there for you, grabbing a **Potion** on your right en route. The enemy party here is made up of three Wutai enemies, a Staff Sergeant and two Soldier Jias. Eliminate the lesser Jias first

(since they're so weak), then concentrate on the Staff Sergeant. Your reward for winning this battle is the Libra materia.

Mission 4-1-4: Wutai Remnants in the Slums

Enemies: Wutai Soldier Jia, Balo Balo, Wutai Staff Sergeant
Objective Party: Balo Balo, Wutai Staff Sergeant (x2)
Prize: Muscle Belt
Information: "An escaped Wutai trooper is hiding in the slums of Midgar. He seems to have joined with an anti-Shinra element based in the slums, planning a strike against the Shinra Building. You must quickly eliminate the threats before they have a chance to make their move."
Notes: This mission is a relatively easy one. Simply run forward from the starting position, and almost immediately you'll see the enemy party waiting for you ahead. Before you go forward all the way to engage them, however, be certain that you grab the **Thunder Materia** from the slightly-obscured treasure chest on your right. Then, head forward to the enemies waiting. The party will be made up of a Balo Balo and two Wutai Staff Sergeants. The Balo Balo is by far the bigger threat, so concentrate on him first, trying to flank him if possible for extra damage. Then turn your attention on the simplistic Wutai Staff Sergeants. When all are slain, a Muscle Belt is yours.

Mission 4-1-5: Stop the Intruders

Enemies: Wutai Corporal, Wutai Soldier Yi
Objective Party: Wutai Corporal, Wutai Soldier Yi (x6)
Prize: Mute Shock
Information: "Most of the Wutai remnants hiding in the slums have been suppressed, but a group has slipped through Shinra's Building. Eliminate all Wutai fighters in the city streets."
Notes: Sadly, this map can get you a little turned around, especially because there are quite a few items to grab en route to the objective party. The first thing you want to do after gaining control here is to turn around and find the **Barrier Materia**. Then, head forward until you reach a fork, where you can go left or right. Head right, following the linear pathway until you can continue straight or go left. Go left first, following that passageway to grab an **Elixir**, then rejoin the path and continue along to the only other unexplored part of the map. At the end of this path is the boss party (grab the **Potion** en route). The enemy party is numerous, but nothing too powerful. You'll actually be fighting these enemies in the dungeon leading up to this fight, so you should be plenty prepared for what they bring.

Mission 4-1-6: Search for Wutai Remnants

Enemies: Wutai Soldier Bing, Wutai Sergeant Major
Objective Party: Vajradhara Cala
Prize: Poison Blade
Information: "Information from several sources points to the existence of Wutai remnants in Fort Condor. Although facts cannot be confirmed at this time, it seems entirely feasible. Go to Fort Condor and conduct an investigation.
Notes: This final mission on the "Pursue the Remnants" chain poses a considerable challenge, not in the regular enemies present (though they are tough, in the form of Wutai Soldier Bings and Wutai Sergeant Majors) but in the boss battle with Vajradhara Cala. The path leading up to this battle is linear in nature -- just be sure to veer off the path to grab the **Potion** and **Hi-Potion** (both are en route to the boss on the left side, slightly obscured by rocks and the like). The battle with Vajradhara Cala will test your stamina, because he has a lot of hit points. Doing him in won't be an easy feat, especially because he has a powerful and unavoidable attack called the Tomahawk Boomerang. Regardless, it's his hit HP that makes him most

annoying, but thankfully his slow speed allows you to get behind him to inflict critical damage with regularity. Doing so will make this battle much more manageable.

04-02: Behind the Scenes

Mission 4-2-1: Foes in the Corel Mines

Enemies: Wutai Soldier Bing, Wutai Sergeant Major
Objective Party: Vajradhara Cala
Prize: Lightning Armlet
Information: "A group of Wutai remnants, different from the ones we were pursuing before, is massing in the Corel Mines. Go to Corel immediately and stop the remnants in their tracks."
Notes: Head forward from the starting area. When you come to a branch heading to your left, ignore it, as it ultimately leads to a dead end with nothing of interest. Instead, push forward, grabbing the **Titanium Bangle** from the treasure chest on your right, and then head left along the linear pathway. You'll soon see your target enemy party ahead waiting for you on a bridge, but be sure to head to your right, down a dead end pathway. There's a **Muscle Belt** there. Then, backtrack to the boss. This enemy is a Vajradhara Cala, which if you're on this mission you've already fought and defeated before. Remember that because of their high HP, getting behind them for critical damage is a good idea, though you'll have little room to maneuver here.

Mission 4-2-2: Remnants in the Slums

Enemies: Wutai Soldier Bing, Wutai Sergeant Major, Vajradhara Cala
Objective Party: Wutai Sergeant Major, Vajradhara Cala
Prize: Gold Armlet
Information: "Wutai remnants are hiding in the slums again. They have joined forced with other anti-Shinra elements, but now have large anti-SOLDIER weapons in their arsenal. Eradicate them before they make a move."
Notes: This area is, in essence, a giant circle. Begin by going forward and navigating leftward around the circle. You'll meet familiar enemies from previous missions here, but annoyingly enough, Vajradhara Cala enemies are now fair game outside of boss battles, so be prepared. The first chest you'll encounter on your left will contain an **AP Up+ Materia**. Once you grab it, backtrack towards the entrance and this time take the right part of the circle. A chest will be on your left eventually, this one holding an **X-Potion**. Further up the circle is the boss party. The Vajradhara Cala here will be accompanied by a Wutai Sergeant Major. Nothing too bad here, but the Sergeant Major should be your first target simply because of his significantly less HP and pesky Shoot skill.

Mission 4-2-3: Foes inside Shinra Building

Enemies: Wutai Soldier Ding, Bajang, Wutai Sergeant Major
Objective Party: Vajradhara Rakshasa
Prize: Blaze Armlet
Information: "The Wutai remnants in the slums were decoys. A detached unit has entered the basement level of the Shinra Building. Head to the site immediately and eradicate the Wutai remnants."
Notes: Head forward from the entrance and immediately turn left to find two **Power Stones** in a treasure chest there before continuing rightward. The pathway is completely linear until you reach a square-shaped segment, which will allow you to go either right or left. First, turn and face the doorway into this area to find two **Mind Stones** in a treasure chest. Then, take either branch, as they both lead to the same place on

the other side of the square (the smaller square within this square has nothing of interest, so ignore it). Grab the three **Guard Stones** from the chest as you veer off of the path and towards the objective party. The enemy here is one you've never encountered, a Vajradhara Rakshasa. Similar to his cousins, he's slow and powerful, so get behind him for critical attacks and dodge his attacks, curing constantly if he's damaging you. His special attack, Magnitude 8, can't be avoided however. Whenever he uses it, heal immediately.

Mission 4-2-4: March into Wutai

Enemies: Bajang, Wutai Soldier Ding, Wutai Captain
Objective Party: Vajradhara Indra
Prize: AP Up++ Materia
Information: "With the Wutai remnants eliminated from Midgar, Shinra troops are gearing up to march into Wutai and hunt down any remnants of anti-Shinra elements. SOLDIER will provide support in this operation. Head for Wutai and attack the anti-Shinra base."
Notes: Taking a look at the map of this area will reveal its complexity. From the starting point, you'll want to head due south, not veering off of the path. You'll find a **Muscle Belt** on your left almost immediately as you do so. Once you grab it, backtrack a bit and head down the horizontal path we just told you to ignore. Keep going until you can't go anymore and are forced rightward. You'll find two more treasure chests here right next to each other. One contains a **Hi-Potion** and the other some **SPR Up+ Materia**. Then go forward and left to engage the primary enemy party. This foe is a Vajradhara Indra, which you've likely not encountered before. Like his cousins, he's slow moving, and he also uses the Mace Boomerang attack with loyal regularity (it's impossible to avoid). It's vital that you heal constantly and get behind him for critical attacks. His high HP means this battle will last a really long time if you don't do so.

Mission 4-2-5: Stubborn Wutai Remnants

Enemies: Vajradhara Indra, Wutai Soldier Ding, Bajang
Objective Party: Vajradhara Indra, Bajang
Prize: Sprint Shoes
Information: "While Shinra troops have crushed one Wutai remnant base after another, one has maintained its resistance and fends off any Shinra attack. The Shinra troops have asked for SOLDIER's assistance. Head there immediately and crush the base."
Notes: This long cavernous corridor is almost impossible to get lost on en route to the objective party, but you'll be fighting some tough enemies. You've dealt with the Wutai Soldier Dings and Bajangs before, no doubt, but you haven't fought Vajradhara Indras as regular enemies encountered via random encounters. They're annoying and they *spam* their Mage Boomerang over and over again, so keep healing as needed. There are two items of interest to grab as you head to the objective party's location -- an **Elixir** on a treasure chest on the left side of the path, and a **Gravity Materia** located in a little nook on the left as you swing right towards the Vajradhara Indra and Bajang, which are this mission's objective party. Make sure to take out the Bajang first. He's not only much easier to kill, but his Firaga spell is really annoying. Then focus on the Vajradhara Indra, and remember -- stay well-healed. The Boomerang Mace attack is no joke.

Mission 4-2-6: The Five Saints of Wutai

Enemies: Wutai Soldier Ding, Wutai Captain, Bajang
Objective Party: Crescent Unit Primus, Crescent Unit Tertius, Crescent Unit Secundus, Crescent Unit Auintus, Crescent Unit Quartus
Prize: Wutai Secret Shop
Information: "Wutai remnants are apparently under orders from entities dubbed the Five Saints of Wutai. Defeating them would put an end to our conflict with the remnants. Sneak into their base, and eliminate the Five Saints of Wutai."

Notes: Head forward from the starting point. As the path turns, be sure to grab a whopping **5,000 Gil** from the treasure chest. The path will eventually open up into a much larger area that's shaped like a square. Stay against the left wall as you go in. This will allow you to grab the **Drain Blade** out of the chest there. Then, head into the square, where in each quadrant, you'll find a different enemy. Each of these enemies represents four of the five separate objective battles here, which are all one-on-one battles (the fifth enemy is down the path at the north end of this area). Thankfully, each enemy fights the same way, and all of them are pushovers so long as you remember that by continuously attacking them, they'll never get a chance to attack back. They have three main attacks. AP Spiller, which doesn't damage you but rather takes some AP from you, Jagged Edge, which is an easy-to-dodge melee attack, and Anesthetic Missile, which is perhaps the biggest pain of them all, since it temporarily paralyzes you. They can also cast Curaga on themselves. So, keep the attacks going, and they won't even get a chance to respond. How nice! You'll get access to a brand new shop chock full of powerful materia for your victory.

05-01: Sample Monsters Lv.1

Mission 5-1-1: Experiment No. 101

Enemies: None.
Objective Party: Ifrit
Prize: Fire Materia
Information: "Your battle with the summon made for valuable data. I have used this data to create a new battle sim; be my guest and give it a try if you're up to it. But I must warn you--though it is only a simulation, the damage you receive will be very real."
Notes: By the time you're able to undertake this particular mission, you would have already fought and defeated Ifrit during the Wutai campaign early in our journey. This Ifrit is the same monster. Blizzard works extremely well on him, but his powerful attacks (like Hellfire) necessitate a bob-and-weave technique. Keep rolling and blocking his attacks, get in your own melee attacks coupled with Blizzard, and most importantly, stay healed. You'll win with these techniques, adding Fire Materia to your inventory as a result.

Mission 5-1-2: Experiment No. 102

Enemies: None.
Objective Party: Bahamut
Prize: Amulet
Information: "Bahamut! A rare find, indeed... I thank you for such an invaluable sample. I have created another battle simulation based on this data, so have at it once you're ready."
Notes: By the time you're eligible to undertake this mission, you would have already fought Bahamut. So, you'll know precisely what to expect, except you should be a little stronger this time around, and well-aware of what to expect. Bahamut can slash at you with his claws, but his two primary attacks are a jumping attack, which shakes the ground and is impossible to dodge (though you can block it), and Mega Flare, an unavoidable fire spell that can obliterate you (so be quick on the healing). Otherwise, Bahamut was once a formidable foe that just isn't by the time you fight him in this mission. Mega Flare or not, you should have little difficulty taking him down.

Mission 5-1-3: Experiment No. 103

Enemies: A-Ahriman, A-Sahagin
Objective Party: A-Ahriman (x2), A-Sahagin (x2)
Prize: Lightning Ring

Information: "I already know it's a failure, so I'm not especially keen on this... but I did recreate an Angeal copy based on combat intel. It's just a monster with a little bit of intelligence. On second though, it's probably a perfect match."

Notes: Unlike the first two missions in this chain, you'll actually have to traverse a dungeon during the mission before reaching the objective party. Stranger yet is the fact that the only enemies you'll encounter are the same enemies in the objective party -- A-Ahriman and A-Sahagin. Both of these foes are pushovers, and any preparation you need in how they fight will be given to you plenty as you travel through this linear dungeon to the far, far side of it, where the objective party is located. A-Sahagin is a melee fighter, while his airborne friend, the A-Ahriman, cast spells and attacks from afar.

Mission 5-1-4: Experiment No. 104

Enemies: None.
Objective Party: Bahamut Fury
Prize: Drain Materia
Information: "A very intriguing sample. A Bahamut strain! Genesis has more than a few tricks up his eleeve. So, this is a simulated battle--with special thanks to Genesis. Allow me to collect more combat data while you dish out the hurt."

Notes: We're back to what seems to be the normal way we'll be fighting through many of Hojo's experiments -- immediately, and without having to work our way to them. You'll remember Bahamut Fury from the game's main quest, since he'll only be unlocked to battle here once you fought him there. Unlike virtually all enemies in the game, Bahamut Fury won't move and can't be flanked (so there's no delivering critical damage here unless the DMW bestows that upon you). So, rush him and begin dealing damage the old-fashioned way, taking care to dodge his swipe attacks. Certain skills like Hexafang are more difficult to avoid, but other than Megaflare, he won't throw much at you that can't be dodged outright. His size is daunting, and he looks really mean, but believe it or not he shouldn't challenge you too badly once you encounter him here. After all, you've already fought him and defeated him once, right?

06-01: Looking For Items

Mission 6-1-1: Closed Coal Mines

Enemies: Fly Eye, Spriggan
Objective Party: Fly Eye (x2), Spriggan
Prize: Phoenix Down
Information: "We have obtained information on monsters dwelling in the closed coal mines. There is a possibility that the mines were shut off with precious items still inside. Please go investigate."

Notes: From your starting location, run forward into the cave, and bear leftward. You'll see a treasure chest there -- obtain a **Hi-Potion** from it. Then, continue along the linear pathway until you reach a larger cavern where a Spriggan appears to be waiting for your arrival. As you approach, two of his Fly Eye friends will appear. Thankfully, both of these foes are of a variety you'll fight in random encounters during this mission, so you should know what to expect. Fly Eyes are *much* more powerful than Spriggans, so concentrate on them, since the Spriggan will likely die during the engagement simply by being hit with stray attacks. And also, dodge the Fly Eye's and Spriggan's spells.

Mission 6-1-2: Desert Island Delights

Enemies: Fly Eye, Spriggan, Raijncho
Objective Party: Fly Eye (x2), Raijncho (x2)

Prize: Chocobo Armlet
Information: "We have obtained information on monsters living on a desert island. You may also be able to find some items there. Please go investigate."
Notes: From the outset, head forward down the linear pathway. As it winds leftward, you'll run into a treasure chest containing an **Elixir**. Once you've obtained that and added it to your inventory, you can proceed down the path until you run into an enemy party waiting for your arrival. This enemy party that we must defeat is made up of a pair of Fly Eyes, as well as peskier and more robust airborne enemies known as Raijnchos. The Fly Eyes can poison you, which is annoying, so you'll actually want to concentrate on them first, dodging their spells and the like. Then turn your attention on the friends in flight, who can easily be felled with the proper techniques. You'll attain a Chocobo Armlet, an AP raising accessory, for your troubles.

Mission 6-1-3: Scavenger Hunt

Enemies: Fly Eye, Spriggan, Trap, Raijncho
Objective Party: Raijncho (x3)
Prize: Jump Materia
Information: "Monsters have appeared in the slums. You must eliminate the threats before any of the citizenry are hurt. We ask that you also conduct a thorough investigation of the area."
Notes: From the start, run forward through the slums. The pathway will create a sort of semi-circle with an area going off to the left. First, head forward along the initial semi-circular pathway, where a treasure chest will eventually be located on your right. Open it to find a new Materia, **ATK Up**. Continue along the semi-circle fighting random battles until you see a Raijncho flying in an archway waiting for your arrival. Approach it, first opening the treasure chest on the left to obtain a **Hi-Potion**. Then, engage these foes in combat. You should be ready for what they bring to the table (they cast Thunder a lot). However, you've fought these guys before. This battle should prove to be much the same. Jump Materia is your prize for winning.

Mission 6-1-4: In the Depths of the Caverns

Enemies: Worm, Trap
Objective Party: Worm (x2), Trap
Prize: Dark Matter (x2)
Information: "We have obtained information of monsters dwelling in the caves. You may also be able to find some items there. Please go and investigate."
Notes: Simply run forward from the outset along the linear path. You'll come to a treasure chest on your right as you go -- open it to find a **Silver Armlet**. After acquiring that accessory (which drastically raises your MP, by 40%), swing left down the corridor (going right will give you the option of ending the mission prematurely), and run for the Trap enemy waiting there. As you approach, he'll summon two Worms to help him. This battle can be pesky because the Worms can actually use an attack (called Thread) that will temporarily paralyze you. This can be horrifying if the Trap isn't killed first (since they regularly cast Fira), so kill the Trap first, then concentrate on the Worms. And by all means, dodge Thread as best you can!

Mission 6-1-5: Buried in the Caverns

Enemies: Worm, Mandragora, Trap
Objective Party: Trap (x2), Mandragora (x2), Worm
Prize: Lunar Harp (x2)
Information: "We have obtained information of odd monsters dwelling in the caves. You may also be able to find some items there. Please go and investigate."
Notes: From the outset, head forward along the cavernous pathway until it splits, one direction going right, the other going left. First, bear right to grab the **Fira Materia** from the treasure chest, then go left

around the fork to grab a **Bronze Armlet**. After having both of those items in-hand, continue leftward up the path until you see a Trap enemy hovering above the ground. As you approach him, he'll call some of his friends (another Trap, a Worm and two Mandragoras). The Mandragoras are small, pesky foes that can silence you if you aren't too careful. However, because the Worm can paralyze you, you should make that enemy your first target. Once killed, concentrate on the other foes, and then reap your reward - two Lunar Harps. (You *should definitely* return to this after beating it the "proper" way. When you do, head to the fork and instead of going right, this time go left. Fight the Tonberry you find there (being especially weary of his Kitchen Knife attack). Defeat him to open up more missions elsewhere.)

Mission 6-1-6: Item in the Coal Mines II

Enemies: Replicon, Bizarre Bug
Objective Party: Mandragora (x4)
Prize: Hero Drink (x2)
Information: "We have obtained information on monsters dwelling in the closed coal mines. You may also be able to find items there. Please go and investigate."
Notes: From the start, go forward, and then swing left, and left again along with the linear pathway before you. Simply continue to follow it until you come across a treasure chest on your right (which has **Dark Matter** in it). Further up the linear path (there are *no* ways to get lost here), you'll also find some **Mythril**. After grabbing that, it's a straight-shot to the location of the boss party here (a group of four Mandragoras) who are waiting on a wooden bridge for your arrival. These foes are small in stature, so keep on dodging their attacks and try to group them together so you can hit multiple targets with a single swipe. If they happen to silence you, don't sweat it -- it's nothing a quick Remedy won't fix.

07-01: Recall Missions

Mission 7-1-1: Freight Recall

Enemies: G Assassin, Guard Hound, Heli Gunner
Objective Party: Heli Gunner (x2)
Prize: Headband
Information: "A Shinra freight carrier has sunk near Mideel. Some of its cargo has drifted to a desert island in the area, and the last thing we want is anti-Shinra elements procuring that cargo. Get there and retrieve what is ours."
Notes: As soon as you begin this mission, be certain you turn around to grab the **X-Potion** from the treasure chest there. Then proceed up the path, taking your first right. Head up this innocuous path, grabbing the **Ether** from the treasure chest as the path swings right once more. This will lead to the weak objective party, made up of two easy-to-defeat Heli Gunners. You fight these guys so many times in the regular game that you should know what to do from here.

Mission 7-1-2: Black Market Recall

Enemies: Bee Saucer, G Avenger
Objective Party: Sweeper, Bee Saucer (x2)
Prize: Star Pendant
Information: "Certain Shinra-brand accessories were being traded illegally in the slum marketplace. The employee responsible has already been arrested, but some of the accessories are still hidden in the slums. Go there and recover all of the accessories."

Notes: There's little room to maneuver here, so as soon as you gain control of Zack, start running forward. The objective party and two of the three treasure chests in the area will be immediately visible. The treasure chest on your left heading forward contains a **Soma**, while the chest further up on your right holds an **Elixir**. The objective party is ahead, but hug the left wall going forward to find a **Hi-Potion** in the final chest here. Then engage the objective party in battle. The Sweeper is a tired enemy at this point in the game, one that you should be able to dispatch easily. Its two Bee Saucer companions are even more simplistic.

Mission 7-1-3: Cargo Recall

Enemies: G Assailant, Bee Saucer
Objective Party: Flying Machine, Bee Saucer (x3)
Prize: Diamond Gloves
Information: "Our cargo stolen by an anti-Shinra element has been found inside the plate. The organization was neutralized, but an AI weapon glitch prevented us from reclaiming our precious cargo. We have no use for malfunctioning machines--destroy them and collect our goods!"
Notes: Head downward from your starting point. Going right at both junctures you encounter will lead you to dead ends (or, really, continuations of pathways that aren't available on this particular version of the map), so you'll want to swing left instead when you can. Following the path into the next, linear area, make sure to turn around to find a treasure chest containing **Sprint Shoes** against a door jam. Further up the corridor, a **Power Wrist** can be found along another door jam. The objective party is further up from there. A Flying Machine and three extremely weak (at this point) Bee Saucers should be no problem for anyone in the mid-teens in level or higher. The Flying Machine is mildly stronger than the Sweeper you're more accustomed to fighting, but nothing too notable that will make him much harder.

Mission 7-1-4: Supplies Recall

Enemies: G Commando, Metal Saucer
Objective Party: Metal Saucer (x2), G Commando (x2)
Prize: Pearl Necklace
Information: "SOLDIER supplies that went missing along with stocks of Shinra weapons have been found in the wasteland. Genesis troops have also been spied in the area. Go to the site and collect all supplies."
Notes: From the outset, head forward and then quickly go left as soon as you can. Follow this wall all the way up until you can't anymore. Nearby, you'll see a treasure chest obscured from vision by a large boulder. Open it to acquire an **X-Potion**. Continue along the pathway as it constricts back to a smaller size. This next area is where the objective party is, but hug the leftmost wall (like you did earlier) to find another treasure chest, this one with an **Ice Armlet** within. The objective party is made up of the only two types of enemies you'll fight in this area via random encounters, so you should be well-prepared for this battle. Metal Saucers use the attack Discharge often, but it's easily dodged and they are easily taken care of. G Commandos, on the other hand, use the pesky Devil's Knife, which will Silence *and* Poison you if it connects. That's not good, so dodge that attack all costs (or use a Remedy if it connects). And be quick with them, too, since they can cure themselves by casting Cura.

Mission 7-1-5: Deputy Assignment

Enemies: G Diver, Needle Machine, Guard Fang
Objective Party: Needle Machine, Guard Fang
Prize: Frost Armlet
Information: "A SOLDIER 3rd Class was sent alone to reclaim cargo stolen by Genesis's troops. he came back injured and dejected, and has been pulled out of action. Please ead to the site and collect the cargo."

Notes: Follow the winding, linear pathway -- you'll find some **Blizzara Materia** en route. As the path swings rightward, go forward momentarily towards a corridor you're unable to explore. Nearby, a treasure chest will bear an **Elixir** for you to add to your inventory. Continue along the mostly-linear corridor over a wooden bridge, and grab the **Mythril Gloves** from the chest as the pathway winds away from it. (Keep in mind that the G Divers you meet here use a pesky combo attack called Fin Kick, so if they begin to use it, hit them to make them stop) Eventually, you'll reach a fork in the road, where you can continue forward to the waiting objective party, or head leftward down an alternate path. Take the alternate path first. This will bring you to another wooden bridge, at the end of which an **X-Potion** can be acquired. Then backtrack and opt to take the other pathway towards the objective party. You've dealt with Needle Machines before (the Guard Fang should be nothing more than an afterthought), so you know that their Holy Lance attack should be dodged at all costs. If they hit you with it, be sure to heal yourself quickly. Flanking these enemies to inflict critical damage is your best bet.

Mission 7-1-6: Second Deputy Assignment

Enemies: G Legion, Chain Machine, Launcher Machine
Objective Party: Chain Machine, Launcher Machine
Prize: Sprint Shoes
Information: "This is an emergency situation. Shinra accessories have been stolen by Genesis troops that infiltrated the plate. They are apparently too tough for the SOLDIER 3rd Class operatives we sent in. You must go there and get back the accessories."
Notes: If you take a look at the in-game map of this area, you'll see that you're on the beginning of a pathway which ultimately leads to a square-shaped corridor. This corridor itself goes off in a few directions of interest, but you'll be glad to know that there are no items to find leading up to this area -- just enemies to fight. The corridor and small room on the inside of the square has two treasure chests within, one containing a **Mystile** and the other an **X-Potion**. The room off of the west side of the square has the other two treasure chests in the area, containing a **Hi-Potion** and some **Blizzara Materia**. With those in hand, you can then head to the only unexplored niche of the locale, where a Chain Machine-Launcher Machine combo will be waiting for you. You've dealt with these guys before -- try to eliminate the Launcher Machine first, though, because his Missile attack can be devastating and is almost impossible to dodge (though it can be blocked).

07-02: Precious Things

Mission 7-2-1: Search and Destroy

Enemies: Pile Machine, Sweeper
Objective Party: Sweeper, G Eraser
Prize: Item Fusion Tome
Information: "We have located one of Genesis's underground equipment bunkers. Destroying this facility would put a heavy dent into their reinforcements. Go there immediately, infiltrate the site, crush the enemy, and collect their equipment."
Notes: Head forward from the start (don't worry about the unexplored area behind you -- there's nothing there of interest). When you get to a fork, head right. At the end of this pathway, you'll find **Blizzard Materia**. Grab it, and then go back to the fork and head in the other direction. As you head down this pathway, be sure to grab the **Hi-Potion** from the treasure chest on your left. Before going left down the lengthy pathway there, continue along the route you're on towards the dead end. Two treasure chests can be found on this path, both on your left. One contains another **Hi-Potion**, and the other a **Soma**. After grabbing those items, explore the only unexplored pathway here. At the end of the path is the objective party (be sure to grab the **Remedy** en route). The Sweeper and G Eraser waiting for you here are both

pushovers considering where you should be at the point in the game you unlock this mission. Trust us --
the Pile Machines you meet en route to them are actually much harder.

Mission 7-2-2: Search and Destroy II

Enemies: Sweeper, Cutter Machine, Red Saucer III, G Avenger
Objective Party: Arachno
Prize: Keychain
Information: "We have destroyed their factory, but Genesis troops have built yet another in a new
location. You must raid the site and crush the enemy. However, they have learned from the last attack and
have boosted their defenses. Proceed with caution."
Notes: If you take a look at the map here from the outset, you'll see just how ridiculously extensive this
area is. Begin by heading forward (southward on the map) to the first turn. There are no treasure chests on
that long route south, so don't worry about that. The first left you encounter leads immediately to the
objective party, so ignore it for now and take the next left instead. **MAG Up Materia** can be found din a
chest down there. If you then head to the westernmost part of the map, there's a vertical corridor with a
single treasure chest on either side. Grab the **Gris-Gris Bag** and the **Elixir** from these chests. Explore the
north-bearing pathway hereafter. At the dead end you encounter, the mother load of items can be found.
A **Hi-Potion**, an **X-Potion**, and some **Mythril Gloves** will be found in three chests. Remember where we
said to avoid the objective party earlier? Go back there and do battle with Arachno, a giant robotic spider
you've fought before. He's slow, so you can get behind him to deal critical damage. Just be careful of his
pesky Super EM Field!

Mission 7-2-3: Operation: Mako Reactor I

Enemies: Bizarre Bug, King Scarab
Objective Party: Bizarre Bug (x4), King Scarab (x2)
Prize: Thunder Armlet
Information: "Monsters have appeared in a mako reactor construction site, shutting down several working
blocks. SOLDIER must break through the closed-off blocks, eliminate the swarm of insectoid monsters,
and collect any equipment left on site."
Notes: If you take a look at the map, you'll see a huge horizontal corridor stretching to the east and to the
west that is split by the vertical pathway you start out on. All of the items are found along this horizontal
pathway, but it's a matter of going right (if you're facing the corridor) first, because by doing so, you'll be
able to grab a **Hi-Potion** on your left, and further up on your left an accessory called **Four Slots**. At the
end of this corridor, **Thunder Materia** can be found. Heading in the other direction, grab an **Elixir** and
then approach the objective party, which is made up of six foes total identical to the Bizarre Bugs and King
Scarabs you already fought here. With these guys, there truly are no worries.

Mission 7-2-4: Operation: Mako Reactor II

Enemies: King Scarab, Death Claw, Gargoyle
Objective Party: Gargoyle (x2), Death Claw
Prize: Dragon Armlet
Information: "There's still trouble at the mako reactor construction site. With more types of monsters
than before, we can only depend on SOLDIER. Enter the construction area, eliminate the monsters, and
collect the equipment on site."
Notes: From the outset, turn around and go in the opposite direction from which you start. By following
this dead end pathway to its conclusion, you'll find eight **Magic Stones** and eight **AP Stones**. Not bad for
having played here for just a few seconds! A word on one of the enemies you encounter here, however,
just as an aside. Death Claws are white arachnid-humanoid like foes with quite a few HPs. They are
aggressive and have an attack called Deadly Embrace that should be avoided at all costs. If it hits you,

you'll be paralyzed, so watch out! After grabbing those goods, simply head in the other unexplored direction. **MP Stones**, eight of them, can be found en route to the objective party. The objective party is made up of enemies you'll fight on your way through this dungeon so they shouldn't surprise you much. Stay on your toes with Death Claws and watch out for the powerful attack magic of the Gargoyles, including regular Thundaga and Firaga spells.

Mission 7-2-5: Operation: Mako Reactor III

Enemies: Gargoyle, Ahriman, King Scarab
Objective Party: Ahriman, Gargoyle (x2)
Prize: Backpack
Information: "The chaos at the construction site seems to have settled down. Only one block is still closed--if we can bring this final block under control, our job will be done. Please hurry to the site."
Notes: This place is generally pretty linear, so you'll have a hard time getting lost. Head forward a ways -- you'll run into your first treasure chest on your left which contains eight **Luck Stones** for your inventory. Further up the path, as it swings leftward, you'll find some **Mythril Gloves**. When you get the chance to swing rightward, ignore that path for now (since that's where the objective party is) and instead go forward. Follow this pathway to its conclusion to grab **Guard Stones** and **HP Stones**, eight a piece. They're liberal with the items on this chain of missions, eh? After grabbing those items, backtrack to the pathway we told you to ignore earlier and engage the objective party in battle. Like the last battle, you'll be dealing with two pesky Gargoyles as well as an Ahriman, who uses his Curse Gaze with regularity. Just like the Death Claw's Deadly Embrace, this attack (which curses you) should be avoided at all costs.

Mission 7-2-6: Accessories Recall

Enemies: Ahriman
Objective Party: King Scarab (x2), Griffon
Prize: Paralyzing Shock
Information: "Troops carrying accessories have been attacked by monsters. The troops have made it back, but the accessories were left at the site. You must collect the accessories while battling the monsters in the area."
Notes: For being the final excursion on this mission chain, this place is pretty easy to navigate through. Simply head downward from your current location and head leftward. This will ultimately lead you to a dead end, but en route you will find two items -- a **Champion Belt** on your left as you traverse the pathway, and an **Ice Ring** at the dead end. After grabbing those goods, head back in the other direction, the only other unexplored part of the map. Grab the **Elixir** as the path swings leftward towards the objective party, which is made up of two King Scarabs and a Griffon. Make the weak King Scarabs your first target to dilute their numbers, then concentrate on the pesky Griffon. The Griffon can use some gray magic, such as Barrier and Magic Barrier, which will increase his defense to physical and magic attacks. His two primary attacks, Maser and Feather Shots, are easy enough to dodge however, and since he's so slow moving, getting behind him to inflict critical damage isn't that difficult.

08-01: Starting Out

Mission 8-1-1: Rematch with Ifrit

Enemies: None.
Objective Party: Ifrit
Prize: Ifrit Materia

Information: "As a result of analyzing the materia you obtained in your fight with Ifrit, we have succeeded in trapping the creature--and chances are good that you can get your hands on rare materia. Hurry to the site."

Notes: This is simply a rematch with Ifrit, who you've fought a couple of times already. Therefore, explaining what to expect in this battle is somewhat redundant. Use ice-based spells if you want an easy kill, although he should pose no challenge to you even without spells.

Mission 8-1-2: Raijincho

Enemies: Spriggan, Grashtrike
Objective Party: Raijincho (x3)
Prize: Thunder Materia
Information: "We have received information of materia hidden in the nest of an island-dwelling Raijincho. Go to the island and obtain the materia."
Notes: Go forward along this path, fighting the simple enemies you encounter. As the linear path swings leftward, grab the **Hi-Potion** from the treasure chest. Then, proceed around the next bend, where the objective party can be found. Here, you will fight three Raijinchos, airborne eagle-like enemies with attitude. Try to consolidate these airborne foes so they can be struck simultaneously. This will make them far more manageable.

Mission 8-1-3: Clash with Genesis Troops

Enemies: Guard Hound, Blood Taste, G Avenger
Objective Party: Blood Taste (x2), G Avenger (x2)
Prize: HP Up Materia
Information: "We received word that Genesis troops are currently transporting precious materia they have shamelessly pilfered from Shinra. We take the security of our materia seriously--so get it back!"
Notes: This brief mission is simple enough. From the beginning, head southward and take a left at the fork. Follow this pathway to a dead end, where an **Ether** can be acquired from a treasure chest. Then, backtrack and take the other side of the fork we earlier encountered. There are no more items to grab, so it's a straight shot to the extremely weak objective party made up of a pair of Blood Tastes and a pair of G Avengers, which should take one hit each -- two max -- to kill. Some materia is your prize for winning.

Mission 8-1-4: Rematch with Bahamut

Enemies: None.
Objective Party: Bahamut
Prize: Bahamut Materia
Information: "We thoroughly analyzed the materia you retrieved during your fight with Bahamut, and we believe we have isolated his current location. Hurry to the site--chances are good that you can get your hands on some more rare materia."
Notes: We won't waste your time with yet another example on how to beat Bahamut. This is likely the *third* time you've fought him in the game, so you should be plenty prepared for what he brings to the table. His only real attack of consequence is the unavoidable Mega Flare, but other than that, you should be in the clear for easy victory. Bahamut Materia, a very awesome acquisition indeed, is your prize for defeating him yet again.

Mission 8-1-5: Escape from Hojo's Lab

Enemies: Replicon, Bat Eye
Objective Party: Epiornis, Replicon
Prize: Regen Materia

Information: "A monster has escaped from Hojo Laboratories. The monster has been powered up by materia and must be captured at any cost! Hunt it down, and take its materia after it has been subdued."
Notes: These wide open field missions are a bit of a pain because finding any possible treasure requires quite a bit of work. However, as far as we could tell through our playing of the stage, there are no items to worry about. So, you should make your way clear across the map to the objective party, which is made up of a Replicon (which you will fight all over this map) and a stronger version of the ostrich-like foes called Epiornis. Both are relatively easy, and if you attack continuously, they won't even be able to squeak out a response of any kind. That makes this battle *quite* easy no matter when you're undertaking it.

Mission 8-1-6: Mystery Materia

Enemies: Bizarre Bug, Mandragora
Objective Party: Hungry
Prize: Odin Materia
Information: "We detected a strong materia reaction in the caves. Its source is unknown, as there appears to be no presence of Genesis copies or Wutai remnants. No mako eruptions have been reported either, so conduct an investigation immediately."
Notes: From the outset, turn around and head to the dead end behind you. Acquire the **Fire Armlet** waiting for you there, and then turn around and go in the direction you were originally facing. It's all linear from here, so simply take the only unexplored path to its conclusion (grabbing the **Potion** as you go). The objective party is a lone enemy called Hungry, who is a slow, dim-witted enemy that's extremely easy to kill. Consider hacking and slashing away endlessly to take him out, but avoid his Blizzaga casts and hit devastating Bite attack. You will be thankful to learn, however, that he's quite easy to flank, so dealing critical damage should be no problem for you.

08-02: Mako Stones

Mission 8-2-1: SPR Mako Stone

Enemies: Fly Eye, Spriggan
Objective Party: Fly Eye (x2), Spriggan
Prize: SPR Mako Stone
Information: "A spirit mako stone has been detected in the slums of Sector 6. Mako stones are invaluable as research material for materia generation. Hurry to the slums and obtain the mako stone."
Notes: This is an extremely easy, simply and straight-forward mission regardless of when you decide to undertake it. Simply go forward down the short path towards the waiting enemy party, grabbing the **Potion** from the left as you go. The objective party is made up of two Fly Eyes and a Spriggan. This is easy -- far too easy to necessitate any explanation.

Mission 8-2-2: VIT Mako Stone

Enemies: Fly Eye, Spriggan
Objective Party: Grashtrike (x3)
Prize: VIT Mako Stone
Information: "We have detected a reaction from a vitality mako stone in the suburbs of Mideel. You will most likely encounter monsters in the area. Use caution as you make your way to the mako stone."
Notes: Head forward along the path ahead of you, grabbing the **Potion** from the treasure chest in the high grass as the path swings rightward. The objective party is straight ahead. However, there's a cleverly-placed treasure chest behind the party, so hug the left side of the pathway going forward to grab the **Soma** there

without prematurely triggering the battle. The objective party is made up of three Grashtrikes, weak snake-like enemies you can slay with ease. A VIT Mako Stone is yours for the victory.

Mission 8-2-3: MAG Mako Stone

Enemies: Fly Eye
Objective Party: Raijincho, Grashtrike (x2)
Prize: MAG Mako Stone
Information: "We have detected a reaction from a magic mako stone near Mount Corel. You will most likely encounter monsters in the area. Use caution as you make your way to the mako stone."
Notes: Yes indeed -- yet another extremely short mission that's a no-brainer to get through. You'll find a **Hi-Potion** down the short route towards the objective party, so be sure to grab it before you get too close to the party (so that the battle begins). The enemy party, a basic party of two Grashtrikes and a Raijincho should be a pushover for you, even if you're just starting out.

Mission 8-2-4: HP Mako Stone

Enemies: Raijincho, Bizarre Bug
Objective Party: Bat Eye (x2)
Prize: HP Mako Stone
Information: "We have detected a reaction from an HP mako stone in the plains. You will most likely encounter monsters in the area. Use caution as you make your way to the mako stone."
Notes: You're in another wide open field here, and these places are notoriously annoying and difficult to fluidly explore. So let us help! Turn around from the start and grab the **Ether** from the treasure chest there. Then work your way to the southwest segment of the map, where an **X-Potion** can be found. In the northeast corner, you can find some **MAG Up Materia**, and to the west of that, a **Hi-Potion**. West from there is the objective party. This party is made up of two Bat Eyes, simplistic airborne enemies. You should be able to take them easily -- just be weary of their Silence attack, which can silence you if it connects. And that's just pesky, and will force you to use a Remedy.

Mission 8-2-5: ATK Mako Stone

Enemies: Mandragora, Slaps, Trap
Objective Party: Slaps, Mandragora (x2)
Prize: ATK Mako Stone
Information: "We have detected a reaction from an attack mako stone in the wasteland northeast of Cosmo Canyon. You will most likely encounter monsters in the area. Use caution as you make your way to the mako stone."
Notes: Head forward from the starting point, bearing right with the path as it turns. As the path turns left thereafter, be sure to crack open the treasure chest there to grab a **Phoenix Down**. Then continue forward all the way to a dead end (don't go right down an alternate path yet), where an **X-Potion** can be found. After adding that to your inventory, backtrack to the only unexplored pathway, where the objective party can be found. This party is made up of a pair of Mandragoras and an enemy called Traps, which you no doubt encountered in random encounters here. The Mandragoras are easy enough to kill, but Traps might be difficult for you. They take very little damage from physical attacks, and can both silence you *and* poison you simultaneously. Their weakness? Try a fire spell for a one-hit kill.

Mission 8-2-6: LCK Mako Stone

Enemies: Death Claw, Mandragora
Objective Party: Death Claw (x2), Slaps
Prize: LCK Mako Stone

Information: "We have detected a reaction from a luck mako stone in the Mythril Mines. You will most likely encounter monsters in the area. Use caution as you make your way to the mako stone."

Notes: Considering this is the last mission on this chain, getting from point A to point B is pretty straightforward. Go north with the linear pathway (grabbing the **Fira Materia** en route), and when the path swings leftward, following along the new branch of the path. Before you reach the objective party at the end of the path, you'll find an **Esuna Materia** waiting for you. Throw that in your inventory and then proceed to engage the objective party in battle. Death Claws use attacks that can paralyze you, so you'll want to be extremely careful to dodge what they throw at you. Slaps, on the other hand, is a swarm of bugs. When attacked physically, it won't sustain much damage. Use fire-based magic to take them out extremely effectively.

08-03: To Hell and Back

Mission 8-3-1: EM Hell in the Building

Enemies: Chain Machine, G Legion, Bee Saucer II
Objective Party: Chain Machine, Bee Saucer II (x2)
Prize: Stop Blade
Information: "An abnormal electromagnetic field has been activated in a building, damaging the machinery we planned to use in our site investigation. Shinra troops cannot enter with monsters swarming inside. Find the cause of the abnormality and eliminate it."
Notes: From where you begin, head forward and then swing rightward down the corridor. While going leftward will bring you to the same place ultimately, you'll want to head right instead. This is because off of this side of the corridor, a room can be found which contains a **Dispel Materia** -- simply turn around and face the door once in the room to find it. After grabbing it, continue to the northernmost chamber, where the objective party lays in wait. Made up of a Chain Machine and two Bee Saucer IIs, the Bee Saucers are actually the bigger problem, because they can cast gray magic like Wall and even poison you. Since they are far weaker than the Chain Machine, you should probably prioritize killing them first, since they are easier targets.

Mission 8-3-2: EM Hell on the Island

Enemies: G Legion, Bee Saucer II
Objective Party: Sky Gunner (x2), Bee Saucer II (x2)
Prize: Status Ward
Information: "An abnormal electromagnetic field has been activated on a desert island, damaging the machinery we planned to use in our site investigation. Shinra troops are at a stalemate with monsters swarming the area. Find the cause of the abnormality and eliminate it."
Notes: Head down the linear, winding and rather lengthy pathway from the beginning of this mission. The route won't branch until you're well into the terrain, so be prepared to fight plenty of G Legions and Bee Saucer IIs. When the path does split, going left will bring you to the objective party while going right will bring you to a dead end. The dead end has two treasure chests for you to grab contents out of, however, so grab the **Diamond Gloves** and the **Gravity Materia**, then backtrack and take the left path, grabbing the **Hi-Potion** en route to the objective party. This party is made up of two Sky Gunners and two Bee Saucer IIs. You should be familiar with both types of enemies. If you're having difficulty, spam the foes with lightning-based magic, which will take 'em down quick.

Mission 8-3-3: - EM Hell in the Wasteland

Enemies: Ahriman, Dorky Face

Objective Party: Nightmare, Dorky Face (x2)
Prize: Elemental Strike Materia
Information: "An abnormal electromagnetic field has been activated in the wasteland, damaging the machinery we planned to use in our site investigation. Shinra troops cannot enter with monsters swarming the area. Find the cause of the abnormality and eliminate it."
Notes: Head northward from your starting location, grabbing the **X-Potion** on your left as you go. Turn right when the path bends and you'll see your objective party. Dodge them for now, however, swinging left as you stay against the left wall head northward. If you go left at the next chance, you can find an **Elixir**. Then, backtrack to engage the objective party in battle. The three airborne enemies you have to deal with here are two Dorky Faces and a Nightmare. You should be somewhat familiar with Dorky Faces right now. They can use a devastating attack called Dorky Breath that inflicts you with all sorts of status ailments, so be sure to dodge it as best you can. Nightmare can unleash powerful spells such as Blizzaga and Firaga, although his Nightmare Breath, similar to Dorky Breath, is his most powerful attack. Never relent on the attacking, however, and the enemies will scarce have a chance to respond in kind.

Mission 8-3-4: EM Hell in the Mines

Enemies: Evil Eye, Evilgoyle, Nightmare
Objective Party: Demon, Evilgoyle
Prize: MAG Up++ Materia
Information: "An abnormal electromagnetic field has been activated in the coal mines, damaging the machinery we planned to use in our investigation of the site. Shinra troops cannot enter with monsters swarming the area. Find the cause of the abnormality and eliminate it."
Notes: The lengthy cavernous corridor in which this mission takes place is completely linear, so getting lost here is basically impossible. There's plenty of treasure to grab as you work your way through, however. You'll find some **Diamond Gloves, Gravity Materia**, and an awesome accessory you'll probably want to equip called **Shinra Beta**. After finding those three items, you'll run into the objective party. Try to dodge it though by taking the right path (hug the wall so you don't activate it) and you'll find a **Twisted Headband** at the end of the path. Then, backtrack and engage the objective party, made up of a Demon and an Evilgoyle. These foes are both pesky, because they're fluent in magic and have some absolutely annoying skills, including Drain Touch (which hurts you and heals them). They can also cast all three major black magic spell types, so dodging works. Or better yet, hit them while casting to interrupt. Once one is dead, concentrating on the other is no big deal. The battle is much more difficult when you're dealing with two at a time.

08-04: Materia Hunter Zack

Mission 8-4-1: Suspicious Mail 1

Enemies: Grashtrike, Hedgehog Pie
Objective Party: Hedgehog Pie (x3)
Prize: MBarrier Materia
Information: "This message, from someone who claims to be the "treasure princess," is suspect. You can apparently meet this person if you head for the plains. Please go there and confirm the information's accuracy."
Notes: This mission brings you to an outdoor location that looks a bit like a farmstead. Thorough exploration of the area, especially along the nearby pond and around the farmhouse will net you four items -- a **Potion**, a **Hi-Potion**, a **Chocobo Feather**, and a **Soma**. After grabbing those goods, the objective party adjacent to the farmhouse can be engaged. Three Hedgehog Pies, pushover enemies, will be all that's standing in between you and a new piece of materia.

Mission 8-4-2: Suspicious Mail 2

Enemies: Grashtrike, Hedgehog Pie, Bat Eye
Objective Party: Bat Eye (x3)
Prize: Barrier Materia
Information: "It seems the "treasure princess" has recruited you as an ally. You now have orders to hunt for a treasure in the ravine. We assume you feel bad for making her cry the last time. To curb that guilt, head for the ravine."
Notes: Head forward from the outset and bear leftward with the curving, linear pathway. As you go down this next branch of the path and are given the opportunity to go left again, be sure to grab the **HP Up Materia** from the nearby treasure chest before doing so. As you head down from the chest, you'll reach a fork in the road. Should you go left, or go right? Well first, go right. Go to the end of this path, where some **Jump Materia** can be found. Then, head in the other direction, grabbing the **Circlet** from the treasure chest en route to the objective party. The party, made up of three Bat Eyes, is easy enough to eliminate. Be careful of their silence-inducing attacks, however, which will necessitate a Remedy to cure.

Mission 8-4-3: Suspicious Mail 3

Enemies: Trap, Bizarre Bug, Bat Eye
Objective Party: Bat Eye, Trap (x2)
Prize: HP Up+ Materia
Information: "The orders this time (from you-know-who) are to look for a treasure in the plains. We know you're only going along with her to make up for making her cry. She's probably playing you, but if that's okay by you, head for the plains."
Notes: In the wide open field in which this particular mission takes place, you'll start on a path along the western side of the map. Head southward along the very edge of the map (on the west side) to run into some **Stop Materia**. Then, head east along the southern edge of the map to run into an **Ether**. From here, the final two treasures we were able to find in the area -- **Osmose Materia** and **Cait Sith's Megaphone** -- can be found by heading northwest diagonally from the southeastern part of the map. After grabbing those goods, the simplistic objective party made up of a Bat Eye and two Traps can be found. Some new materia is your prize for winning.

Mission 8-4-4: Suspicious Mail 4

Enemies: Guard Fang, G Diver, Crazy Saw
Objective Party: Crazy Saw, G Diver
Prize: Vital Slash Materia
Information: "Our "treasure princess" seems quite upset, though it's obviously not her place to get mad; she's the one providing faulty information. But, if you can act the grown-up and now get cross with her, you can head for the marine caves."
Notes: Head along the linear pathway ahead of you until you reach a fork in the road. You can swing right, or go forward along the same path you're on. Take the left fork, the road you're already on. It leads to the same area the other fork does, but you'll be able to grab an item as you go. The first item you'll come across is **Drainra Materia**. Continue around until you see a path on your left. That's where you have to go to reach the objective party, but ignore it for now. Continue forward to the treasure chest there (containing an **Elixir**) -- this completes the circular pathway we mentioned earlier. With the Elixir in hand, you can then head down the unexplored path back a ways. You'll run into the objective party here, made up of two enemies you'll encounter on your journey through this mission in this area. Be weary of the G Diver's Fin Kick and the Crazy Saw's Drill Attack.

Mission 8-4-5: Suspicious Mail 5</font>

Enemies: Slaps, King Scarab, Dorky Face
Objective Party: Dorky Face (x3)
Prize: MAG Up+ Materia
Information: "The "treasure princess" is threatening to fire you. It must be welcome news for you, but we should make an effort to defend SOLDIER's honor. We suggest you head for the coal mines if only for that reason."
Notes: From the outset, turn around and start running in the other direction. This is a completely linear pathway that will ultimately lead to a dead end, but you'll be able to find a **Silver Armlet** and an **Elixir** down there. Once you grab those items, head back to where you started and go in the direction you were originally facing. Head down this linear pathway until you start running into more treasure -- you'll find a **Mountain Chocobo Armlet** and, as you cross a wooden bridge over a chasm, **Firaga Materia**. Then go forward through the cavern to take on the objective party, made up of three Dorky Faces. These foes are a bit pesky, especially with their Dorky Breath attack, which is a status inflictor. Try to bunch them together so you can get hits on multiple targets simultaneously. This is a simple technique for quick and easy victory.

Mission 8-4-6: Suspicious Mail 6

Enemies: Ahriman, King Scarab
Objective Party: Dual Horn
Prize: Darkness Materia
Information: "You have more orders, and a challenge to a duel, from our "treasure princess." We have had quite enough of this child, so if you're as fed up with her as we are, head for the marine caves and tell her off."
Notes: Head down the pathway ahead of you, grabbing the **VIT Up+ Materia** and the **X-Potion** you encounter en route. When you reach a fork in the road, take the left path first. At the end of this path, you'll find a **Diamond Bracelet**. Grab that, then head down the other end of the fork towards the objective party. The objective party is a gigantic, lone foe named Dual Horn, who you may or may not have already fought in other missions. This foe is slow-moving, making him easy to flank, but his incredibly high defense means that even critical damage isn't much at all. His one major attack (other than goring you with his horns, which creates massive damage on its own) is something called Bad Odor. It's easy to dodge, but if you don't, you'll be cursed, poisoned and silenced simultaneously. Make sure to have a Remedy on-hand just in case.

10-01: Cactoid Secrets

Mission 10-1-1: Where's the Cactuar?

Enemies: Raijincho, Fly Eye
Objective Party: Kactuar
Prize: Muscle Belt
Information: "One of our executives has lost his pet Cactuar. It seems the prickly pet has disappeared with classified company information in its hands. This security breach must be dealt with at once. A door-to-door investigation by Shinra has revealed the Cactuar to be in the wasteland. Exterminate it on sight."
Notes: Strangely, this mission has "Cactuar" spelled in the more traditional C-version, but the enemy you will fight at the end of it all is still Kactuar. If you take a look at the map as you begin, you'll find that you're actually in the middle of an area that can be explored, so your back isn't against a wall or other area that can't be explored as it usually is. You'll want to turn around and explore back there first. There are two pathways that shoot off here, and both have treasure for you (one contained an **Elixir** and the other a **Potion**). Once you've acquired those items, you can then go back to where you began and head in the other direction. There are two more paths in this area, and one leads to a dead end. The other, however,

leads to the objective party, a lone, weak Kactuar. Lay into him to defeat him, and you'll get the Muscle Belt as a prize.

Mission 10-1-2: Kactuar?

Enemies: Kactuar, Trap, Raijincho
Objective Party: Kactuar (x3)
Prize: Champion Belt
Information: "The Cactuar found in the last mission was only a look-alike. Another thorough investigation by Shinra has revealed the Cactuar to be in the wasteland. This one has got to be our executive Cactuar! Exterminate it immediately!"
Notes: Just like during the last mission, your back won't be against a wall or anything of that nature, so backtrack a ways to the end of the corridor behind you. A **Remedy** can be found in a treasure chest there. Once you've grabbed it, returned to where you started and go in the opposite direction. As you head along this linear corridor, take the first right you can to find an **AP Up Materia** before rejoining the path. Take the first left you can (as the objective party is ahead, but we haven't acquired all the treasure here yet). Simply follow this linear, lengthy branch of the path to its conclusion, where a powerful **Cursed Ring** can be found. Then, backtrack and explore the only part of the area where haven't yet, where the objective party is located. This time, you'll have to do battle with not one or two, but three Kactuars. Thankfully, they're pushovers, but you've already realized that by now, haven't you?

Mission 10-1-3: Cactuar Found?

Enemies: Kactuar, Trap, Replicon
Objective Party: Kactuer
Prize: Cactus Thorn
Information: "If we leave things as is, it is only a matter of time before sensitive information is leaked and heads roll. We must, for the sake of these heads, find the Cactuar at all costs. Further investigation has determined its location to be in the wasteland. There is no time to lose!"
Notes: Head forward from the outset, and the path will soon split. First, head left to the dead end, where a **Safety Bit** is hiding away in a treasure chest. Then, go back to the fork and take the previously-unsearched path. The objective party can be seen ahead on the path, but swing left when you can and explore this bit of pathway first. At its conclusion, another treasure chest can be found, this one with a **White Cape**. Finally, backtrack to the pathway yet chosen, which leads to the objective party. Before engaging in battle, though, hug the right wall and continue past the waiting enemy. At the end of that short pathway is the final item here, an **X-Potion**. Once you've gotten all of that, you can then take on the objective party. This foe looks like a Kactuar, but notice the subtle spelling change - he's a Kactuer. This foe is basically just a stronger version of his weaker cousins, but is still nothing at all to worry about. His Cactus Thorn is yours once he's slain.

10-02: Tonberry Quests

Mission 10-2-1: Find the Tonberry!

Enemies: Worm
Objective Party: Tonberry
Prize: Silver Armlet
Information: "Our president's personal chef has requested that we reclaim his prized knife of legend. Investigation has revealed that a Tonberry in the coal mines is currently in possession of the knife. Defeat the Tonberry and claim the cutlery!"

Notes: From the outset, head forward along this linear pathway crawing with Worm enemies (be careful of their paralyzing Thread attacks!) When you get to a fork in the road, first go forward to retrieve **Blizzard Materia** from the treasure chest. Then, backtrack slightly and head up the alternate path nearby. Go over the bridge and continue along this new linear pathway, until you run into the Tonberry you were ordered here to eliminate. Remember that the Tonberry has some weird special attacks, including Karma and knife-based thrusts. However, with only one of them present, he shouldn't present a challenge even to a novice player.

Mission 10-2-2: Tonberries Everywhere

Enemies: Tonberry
Objective Party: Tonberry (x4)
Prize: Gysahl Greens
Information: "The kitchen knife possessed by the previous Tonberry was not the chef's legendary knife. But we have new information about another Tonberry with the chef's precious cutlery. Hurry there and defeat the Tonberry."
Notes: Go forward from the start point along the linear pathway. When you can head right or left at a fork, you'll quickly realize that right is the proper direction in which to head (since left is a dead end). Follow along this next branch of the cavernous area we're in, where you'll find an **X-Potion** in a treasure chest on the left as the pathway opens up into more of a room. The corridor will thin back to its normal size as you continue, but as you reach the dead end at the end of the pathway, you'll fight the boss battle for this mission. You fought Tonberries leading up to this area, but here you'll fight four at the same time. As usual, trying to consolidate the enemies to hit more than one at a time is beneficial, as is getting behind them to deal critical damage. Be weary of their Karma attack (dash away if they begin to use it to avoid being damaged) and if they wield their Kitchen Knife attack, stand away, as it's their most damaging attack.

Mission 10-2-3: Master Tonberry

Enemies: Tonberry, Magic Pot
Objective Party: Master Tonberry
Prize: Tonberry's Knife
Information: "Despite the number of Tonberries in the last mission, not one held the chef's legendary knife. But the latest news is the most reliable yet. The Master Tonberry in the caves is in possession of it! Go slay the Master Tonberry!"
Notes: If you take a look at your map, you'll see that you start in the middle of a winding series of pathways. You have the option, therefore, to head in a northward or southward direction. The northward direction *isn't* where the objective party is located, but you'll want to head in that direction first. By following the linear pathway north, then east, then south to its conclusion, you should encounter two treasure chests -- one with a **Phoenix Down** and one with an **X-Potion**. Then, backtrack all the way to where you began and opt to go in the other direction. When you get to a fork, first head right, since there's more treasure down there. Grab the **X-Potion**, then go back to the fork and take the other path.
A **Mystile** can be found en route to the objective party, made up of a lone Master Tonberry. This foe is just like his Tonberry friends, but stronger. His Kitchen Knife technique is also about three times more potent (plus he disappears before using it). Stay healed and attempt to flank him for critical damage for an easy victory.

10-03: Treasure Hunter Zack

Mission 10-3-1: Items in the Plains

Enemies: King Scarab, Bomb
Objective Party: King Scarab (x2), Dual Horn
Prize: Fat Chocobo Feather (x2)
Information: "Monsters possessing items that can be used as catalysts for materia fusion have been found in the plains. We wish to exactly determine the types of items and monsters present. Go to the site, bash the monsters, and collect the items."
Notes: If you take a look at the map of this area, you'll realize it's a wide open field. However, you'll be sequestered to a certain part of it, so getting lost is unlikely. You'll ultimately want to head to the northwest part of the map in order to fight the boss party, though you'll likely run into Bombs and King Scarabs en route. The boss party is made up of two King Scarabs and a Dual Horn. Take out the King Scarabs as soon as you can, since they are by far the lesser of the enemies. Dual Horn is slow-moving but extremely powerful. You'll want to avoid his Bad Odor attack, but even more than that, avoid his regular headbutt attack, which can do over 2,000 HP in damage (we were at level 22 at the time). He's also got ridiculous defense, so make sure to flank him for critical damage continuously.

Mission 10-3-2: Desert Island Surprises

Enemies: King Scarab, Pachyornis, Dorky Face
Objective Party: Pachyornis (x2)
Prize: Adamantite (x2)
Information: "On a tropical island, we discovered a monster that drops items which are usable in materia fusion. We need more details on both the monster and the items. Head for the island, take down the monster, and grab the items."
Notes: From the outset, head forward along the path you're on. As it swings left, be sure to grab the **Bronze Armlet** from the nearby treasure chest. Then, head right as the path swings again. You'll see the objective party ahead, but you'll want to avoid them at all costs right now -- hug the wall to the right and continue along this alternate path. It's lengthy and it leads to a dead end, but you'll encounter two treasure chests, one containing a **Hi-Potion** and the other a **MAG Up+ Materia**. Once you've acquired those, you can then engage the objective party in battle (the other path away from them is a dead end with no goods). These ostrich-looking foes called Pachyornis are extremely annoying. They're aggressive and they have pecking attacks that can do even a well-leveled for a couple thousand in damage. Try to separate them so that you can take one at a time, but don't be afraid of running away and healing often in this battle. For some reason, these enemies are downright annoying.

Mission 10-3-3: An Item for Fusion

Enemies: Pachyornis, Dorky Face, King Scarab
Objective Party: Pachyornis (x2), Mine (x2)
Prize: Dark Matter (x3)
Information: "Every good SOLDIER operative who wants to power up his materia needs items that can act as catalysts in materia fusion. Therefore, we have established an item search program. We have searched our database and found a location where quality items can be found. Please head there immediately."
Notes: This is one of those obnoxious wide open fields with little direction as far as where you're supposed to go. That's not too much of a worry, however, since we couldn't find any treasure chests here, meaning there's not likely many items you should be worried about. Instead, seek out the objective party immediately, which is made up of two Pachyornis, like we fought before, in addition to two Mines, which are strong Bomb-like enemies. Pachyornis, like before, should be isolated and fought individually, and should be your primary target before moving on to the Mines. The Mines themselves are pesky, but as they make themselves bigger and bigger, they'll eventually self-destruct in an attempt to take you with 'em. So when this happens, get away from them and let them kill themselves. Some Dark Matter will be your prize.

ESSENTIAL SIDE QUEST MISSIONS

Story-Adjacent Missions

This table logs all the Missions you should consider completing as you play through the main story. These have been selected primarily for their rewards: during the main story of the game, they'll often reward useful Materia, Accessories, upgrades, and particularly Summons.

Chapter 2: Embrace Your Dreams

Mission Name	How to Unlock	Why?
M8-1-1: **Rematch with Ifrit**	Complete Chapter 2	Rewards the Ifrit Materia, unlocking him as a Summon.
M4-1-5: **Stop the Intruders**	Complete the preceding M4-1 Missions.	Has a Chest containing the Barrier Materia, which reduces damage from Physical attacks.
M8-2-5: **ATK Mako Stone**	Talk to the scientist in the Materia Room, then complete the preceding Missions.	Allows you to get the Poison and Gravity Materia from the Materia Room scientist.
M10-2-3: **Master Tonberry**	Find the Tonberry in Mission 6-1-5: Buried in the Caverns	Rewards Tonberry's Knife, adding the Tonberry Summon.

Chapter 3: Betrayal?

Mission Name	How to Unlock	Why?
M8-1-3: Clash with Genesis Troops	Complete Chapter 3	Rewards an HP Up Materia.

Mission Name	How to Unlock	Why?
M10-1-3: Kactuar Found?	Find the Cactuar in M3-1-3, then complete the preceding M10-1 Missions.	Rewards the Cactus Thorn, adding the Cactuar Summon.
M8-1-4: Rematch with Bahamut	Complete M8-1-3: Clash with Genesis Troops	Rewards the Bahamut Materia, adding him as a Summon.
M8-1-6: Mystery Materia	Complete the preceding M8-1 Missions.	Rewards the Odin Materia, allowing him as a Summon.

Chapter 4: Monster

Mission Name	How to Unlock	Why?
M8-4-1: Suspicious Mail 1	Enter Mako Reactor 5 during Chapter 4	Rewards the Chocobo Feather, adding the Chocobo Summon.
M8-4-3: Suspicious Mail 3	Complete the preceding M8-4 Missions.	Rewards Cait Sith's Megaphone, adding him as Summon.
M8-4-4: Suspicious Mail 4	Complete M8-4-3: Suspicious Mail 4	Rewards the Moogle's Amulet, adding the Moogle Summon.

Chapter 5: An Angel's Dream

Mission Name	How to Unlock	Why?
M7-2-1: Search and Destroy	Start Chapter 5	Rewards the Item Fusion Tome, allowing you to use Items in Materia Fusion to create Materia with higher stats than normal.
M7-2-2: Search and Destroy II	Complete M7-2-1: Search and Destroy	Rewards the Keychain, allowing Zack to equip three Accessories.
M-7-2-5: Operation: Mako Reactor III	Complete the preceding M7-2 Missions.	Rewards the Backpack, allowing Zack to equip four Accessories.
M6-2-1: Slum Development Plan 1	Talk to the City Planning Director in the Shinra Building Entrance.	Rewards the Sec.8 Materia Shop, stocking HP / MP / AP Up, Drain and Osmose Materia.
M6-2-3: Mako Excavation Site	Complete the preceding M6-2 Missions.	Unlocks the Sec.5 Materia Shop, which stocks various stat Up Materia, and Poison / Silence.
M6-2-6: Underground City	Complete the preceding M6-2 Missions	Unlocks the Sec.6 Accessory Shop, which stocks various Accessories for Materia Fusion.

M4-3-6: **Stop the Assailants**	Complete the Wutai Spy side quest.	Rewards The Happy Turtle shop, stocking mid-tier Materia such as Fira, Regen and Dash.
M4-2-6: The Five Saints of Wutai	Complete the preceding M6-1 and M6-2 Missions	Rewards the Wutai Shop Secret Address, stocking advanced Materia spells.

Endgame Missions

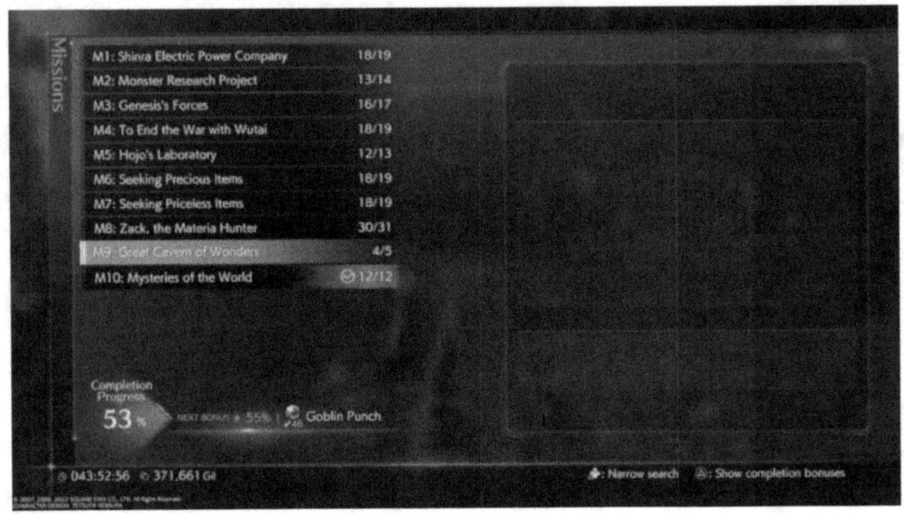

These Missions are exclusively for those who are at the end of Crisis Core's story and intend to 100% the game. They are primarily selected due to their rewards and loot, fully preparing Zack for all Missions ahead, particularly Minerva. You'll be able to access all Missions by the time you clear Chapter 10: See You Soon.

Many of these items can be found in multiple places, however we've listed when you can find them "earliest", according to their Mission designation.

M2: Monster Research Project

Mission Name	How to Unlock	Why?
M2-3-1: **Unidentified Monsters**	Clear M2-2-6: World of Monsters	**Gongaga Trading**: Sells various expert Accessories.
M2-4-1: **A Solitary Island**	Clear M2-3-6: Operation: Desert Island	**Junon Souvenirs**: Sells Materia that increases the likelihood of "Mascot" Summons.
M2-4-5: **Cave-In Investigation**	Clear preceding M2-4-5 Missions.	**Mythril Mine Traders**: Sells Accessories that enable buffs such as Barrier, Regen and Endure.

Mission Name	How to Unlock	Why?
M2-5-1: Investigation of the Caverns	Clear M2-4-6: Whatever Stands in Your Way.	**Element Blade**: Adds Fire, Ice and Lightning to melee attacks.
M2-5-3: More Species Found	Clear preceding M2-5 Missions.	**Wizard Bracelet**: absorbs Fire, Ice and Lightning attacks.
M2-5-6: The Great Beast	Clear preceding M2-5 Missions	**Sniper Eye**: All of Zack's attacks are Critical Hits. **Ribbon**: Prevents all Status ailments (excluding Death). Steal from a Great Malboro.

M3: Genesis's Forces

Mission Name	How to Unlock	Why?
M3-5-4:Chase the Copies	Clear preceding M3-5 Missions.	**Force of Nature**: Fire, Ice and Lightning added to Zack's melee attacks, and absorbed from enemy attacks. Steal this from a G Enforcer.

M4: To End the War with Wutai

Mission Name	How to Unlock	Why?
M4-3-6:Stop the Assailants	Catch Wutai Spy #6 in the Slums playground.	**The Happy Turtle**: Sells various advanced Materia like Fira and Cura.
M4-4-3: Infiltration	Clear Preceding M4-4 Missions.	**Sec.7 Shop**: Sells various powerful Accessories.
M4-4-6: Anti-SOLDIER Weapons	Clear preceding M4-4 Missions.	**Moon Bracer**: Adds a persistent Barrier.

M6: Seeking Precious Items

Mission Name	How to Unlock	Why?
M6-2-1: Slum Development Plan 1	Talk to the City Planning Director in the Shinra Building Entrance.	**Sec.8 Materia Shop**: Sells HP, MP and AP Up Materia.
M6-2-3:Mako Excavation Site	Clear preceding M6-2 Missions.	**Sec.5 Materia Shop**: Sells ATK, VIT, MAG and SPR Up Materia.
M6-2-5:Making Phoenix Down	Clear preceding M6-2 Missions.	**Doc's Code**: When HP falls below 25%, a Potion is automatically consumed.
M6-4-4: Hiding in the Wasteland	Clear preceding M6-4 Missions.	**Nibel Accessories**: Sells Status-causing Abilities and Status-preventing Accessories.

Mission Name	How to Unlock	Why?
M6-4-5:Buried in the Plains	Clear M6-4-4: Hiding in the Wasteland	**Shining Bracer**: Adds persistent MBarrier.

M7: Seeking Priceless Items

Mission Name	How to Unlock	Why?
M7-3-1:P's Precognition Lv. 1	Clear M7-2-6: Accessories Recall	**Black Cowl**: Raises AP cap to 99,999.
M7-3-6:P's Precognition Lv. 6	Clear preceding M7-3 Missions.	**Adaman Bangle**: Raises HP cap to 99,999.
M7-4-2: Second Contact	Clear M7-4-1: First Contact.	**Brigand's Gloves**: Steals are 100% successful.
M7-4-6: Breakthrough	Clear preceding M7-4 Missions.	**Dark Agent**: Zero AP costs.
M7-5-3: Girl on the Desert Island	Clear preceding M7-5 Missions.	**Bone Village Commerce**: Sells Materia that increases the likelihood of "Boss" Summons.
M7-5-4: Second Son in the Wasteland	Clear M7-5-3: Girl on the Desert Island	**Power Suit**: Doubles HP, ATK and VIT (but halves MP, AP, MAG and SPR).
M7-6-2:A Recruiter's Close Call	Clear M7-6-1: A Recruiter's Departure.	**Faerie Ring**: Adds persistent Regen.
M7-6-3:A Recruiter in a Slump	Clear preceding M7-6 Missions.	**Protect Ring**: Adds persistent Barrier and MBarrier.
M7-6-4:The Irritated Recruiter	Clear M7-6-3: A Recruiter in a Slump	**Mog's Amulet**: Items dropped or Stolen from enemies are always rare.
M7-6-6:The Irritated Recruiter	Clear preceding M7-6 Missions.	**Genji Shield**: Negates all Status ailments, permanent Barrier and M Barrier. Encounter and appease a Magic Pot to acquire it (requires Genji Glove).

M9: Great Caverns of Wonders

Mission Name	How to Unlock	Why?
M9-2-5:To the Lower Levels	Clear preceding M9-2 Missions.	**Gold Hairpin**: MP cap raised to 9,999.
M9-3-3: Genesis's New Weapons	Clear preceding M9-3 Missions.	**Net Shop Duo**: Sells element-nullifying Accessories and Sniper Eye.
M9-4-4: Machines Gone Haywire	Clear preceding M9-4 Missions	**Precious Watch**: Doubles gil looted from enemies.

Mission Name	How to Unlock	Why?
		Soul of Thamasa: Zero MP costs.
M9-4-5: Only for SOLDIER	Clear M9-4-4: Machines Gone Haywire	**Magic Master**: Zero MP costs (at the cost of halving HP and AP).
M9-4-6: Biomechanical Threats	Clear M9-4-5: Only for SOLDIER	**Genji Glove**: All attacks are Critical Hits, damage cap raised from 9,999 to 99,999.
M9-5-4: Abnormal Power	Clear preceding M9-5 Missions.	**Jeweled Ring**: Doubles item and Materia drops from enemies. **Laurel Crown**: Zero AP costs. **Costly Punch**: Uses a bit of Zack's HP to inflict extremely high damage. **Net Shop Shade**: Sells the Genji Helm that raises the HP and AP cap to 99,999.
M9-5-6: Even Deeper	Clear preceding M9-5-6 Missions.	**Ziedrich**: Halves all incoming elemental damage, and doubles ATK, VIT, MAG and SPR.
M9-6-2: Lowest Tier	Clear M9-6-1: Toughest Monsters.	**Super Ribbon**: Prevents all Status ailments (including Death).
M9-6-6: The Reigning Deity	Clear preceding M9-6 Missions.	**Divine Slayer**: HP, MP and AP caps raised to 99,999 (redundant however as Minerva is the toughest challenge in the game).

M10: Mysteries of the World

Mission Name	How to Unlock	Why?
M10-1-3: Cactuar Found?	Find and kill Kactuar in M3-1-3: Eliminate the Copies, then complete the preceding M10-1 Missions.	**Safety Bit**: Prevents the Death status ailment.
M10-2-3: Master Tonberry	Find and kill Tonberry in M6-1-5: Buried in the Caverns, then clear preceding M10-2 Missions.	**Feather Cap**: HP, MP and AP can Break up to 3x their normal amount.

THANK YOU!

www.ingramcontent.com/pod-product-compliance
Lightning Source LLC
Chambersburg PA
CBHW081349160726
48000CB00010B/3271